STRANGE WOMAN

Take a young, handsome, virile male who doesn't have a nickel but is used to living like a millionaire, place him in Miami Beach where wealthy, sex-hungry widows are a dime a dozen, and the outcome is inevitable: he will give the frustrated women what they want in order to get *what he wants*.

That's what happened to me, David Mason Horne, and it seemed like a Garden of Eden until Felicia Marr, my latest "client," insisted on playing the role of Adam, leaving the part of Eve for me.

Well, I went along with the deal, figuring that once I had her addicted to "fun and games," I would call the tune, only to discover that Felicia wanted a slave, not a lover and would stoop to anything—including violence—to keep me in bondage.

A Dramatic Novel

LOVE ME TONIGHT

James Kendricks

WILDSIDE PRESS

LOVE ME TONIGHT

ONE

I AM WRITING this book in the death cell.

I have been convicted of murder in the first degree by a judge and jury. Though I am innocent of the crime, I have no way of proving it; but keeping in mind the fight for freedom put up by Caryl Chessman and others like him, I hope that by calling attention to my case to find someone—anyone at all, for I am desperate—who may see the truth and convince the authorities of it before it is too late.

It began three years ago in Florida . . .

I was walking down Collins Avenue in Miami Beach.

Forty cents jingled in a pocket of my expensive Appia slacks. It was all the money I had to my name. The keys to my Alfa-Romeo convertible made a pleasant weight in another pocket. I had a wallet—empty—riding one hip and a five-dollar lawn handkershief on the other. I clung desperately to the trappings of wealth, even though I didn't have the money which should go with them.

My father had died three months before, leaving an estate estimated at between eighty and one hundred million dollars, all of which should have gone to me as his sole heir. The only difficulty was, he was not my natural father.

Twenty years ago, when I had been the loneliest inhabitant of any orphanage in Pennsylvania, and only three years old, Randolph Mason Horne had seen me, taken a liking to me, and ordered his attorneys to make out adoption papers. The trouble was, somebody in the law offices of Hathaway, Moncke and Flanders goofed. As a result, there was a flaw in the title of adoption. I had no more claim to the estate of Randolph Mason Horne than I had to the imposing bulk of the Eden Roc which was looming up ahead of me on Collins Avenue in Miami Beach.

I was broke. A pauper. All this was bad enough, but in the past twenty years of being David Mason Horne, I had acquired the tastes of a gourmet and the appetites of a jaded Roman emperor. On forty cents, American, I could scarcely indulge any of them.

Even the gas tank of the Alfa-Romeo was less than a quarter full, which explains why I was walking. Frankly, I walked to hunt a job. Any job. Even if I couldn't indulge my palate with Crépes Suzette in the Fontainebleau, at least I could still wolf down a hamburger at an open-air stand.

So far in my life I'd had only one job. A friend of mine —a classmate at Harvard who had a Mark Continental concession in his home town—paid me one hundred dollars to drive a brand-new car south to Miami every so often. I'd been in Miami for one week and needed gas money to get home on.

Fumbling in the pocket of my glen-plaid jacket, I brought out a crumpled pack of Old Gold filters. The pack was empty. I made sure by running my finger around inside. I figured if I couldn't eat, I could at least smoke.

Forty cents would buy cigarettes, however.

I turned in at a drugstore doorway and collided, full-length, with a woman on her way out. I was aware of girdled softness and Chanel perfume. I reached and caught her elbows, preventing her from doing any worse than teetering on her high heels.

"I've been careless," I told her. "Please excuse me."

She was not a young woman, but there are few young women visitors to Miami Beach. I judged her to be in her early forties, very chic and polished by years of frequenting the best hotels, the finest restaurants, and receiving the very best of service everywhere she went. I knew the type. Wherever my adoptive father had taken me, I had seen women such as this one.

She smiled up into my face. I'm a little over six feet tall. She was small and fleshy and modishly dressed. Her mouth was heavy with lipstick which glistened redly as she ran her tongue over it.

"Well, of course I'll excuse you," she bubbled. "Goodness, neither of us was looking where we were going, so why should I blame you?"

It was a longer speech than the situation called for, and it made me suddenly alert to opportunity. I squeezed her elbows.

"You're very kind," I told her. "If the situation were a little different, I'd invite you to have a drink at the Chez Bon Bon coffee shop. As it is," and I shrugged and looked off down the street, "all I can offer you right now, besides my apology, are cigarettes. And I have to go in and buy those."

Her eyes touched my sports jacket and slacks, the open-throated cotton chambray shirt. It may have been my imagination, but her eyes seemed to harden with suspicion. Then she drew a deep breath and laughed softly as if she'd made up her mind about me.

"I'd like a cigarette," she said.

I went in, put down thirty cents and got a pack of Old Gold filters in exchange. I ripped the seal, opening it. Tapping the pack on my fingers, I held it out to her, glancing down into the vee slash of her blue organza dress as she bent to the match I struck. I saw a black brassiere and full white breasts gently quivering to her movements.

Her eyes came up and saw where I was staring. Her lips curved into a smile. "Can you dance?" she asked suddenly.

"The cha-cha, the meringue, the fish," I informed her, bowing slightly. "You name it, I dance it." At the social accomplishments, I was an expert.

"You sound like—" she began, then shook her head.

I laughed. "Like a gigolo? Well, I'm not. Oh, I admit I may sound like one, but circumstances are against me. It seems to be a trademark of mine. Have you ever heard of Randolph Mason Horne?"

"Of course. I have an estate in Loudoun County, Virginia, not far from his. He died a few months ago, didn't he?"

"He did. I'm his adopted son."

Her eyes went wide as she flushed with embarrassment. "You must think I'm a ninny," she murmured in irritation at herself.

"On the contrary, I find you a most discerning woman. And if you'll forgive the liberty, a very attractive one. It's true Horne was my father—my name is David Mason Horne—but I'm just what I seem to be—a pauper."

"Now you're teasing me."

"It's a long story," I said, smiling disarmingly, giving her an opening if she wanted one. She did. Her arm caught mine and drew me out the door and along the sidewalk toward a parked Fleetwood.

"You're going to tell me all about it, David. Please?"

At the car she fumbled in a handbag for the keys, lifting them and holding them out. "You drive?"

"These days, to make a living. It's one of the few things I do well." I explained about my job chauffering Mark Continentals from New York to Florida, while she slipped into the suicide seat with an exposure of shapely legs in taut blue nylons.

As I eased the big Fleetwood up Collins Avenue she told

7

me something about herself. Her name was Travis, Mrs. Rhoda Travis. She was a widow whose husband had been something of a tycoon in Wall Street and had left her loaded with IBM and AT&T stocks. She could live very handsomely, I understood, on her dividends alone; but she was tired of her kind of life. There was no excitement, no challenge in it. To while away the time, and since she had a certain facility with her slim fingers, she'd opened a hat store in Westport, back home in Connecticut. To her surprise, it made money from the start.

"I came down here to have fun," she said, turning her neatly coiffed head on the back of the car seat to glance at me.

"You came to the right town," I admitted.

She pouted, "I've been here a whole week and I'm bored silly. I eat three meals every day, I swim dutifully in the pool during the mornings and the ocean in the afternoons. At night I sit alone at a table and listen to a comedian make jokes, and watch chorus girls do high kicks before I stumble off to an empty bed. That's fun?"

"I'll level with you," I said frankly. "I have one thin dime in my slacks. If you foot the bills I'll personally guarantee you'll have as much fun as you're game to take."

Her hand came over to rest on my thigh, fingers widespread. My slacks were thin and her palms seemed to burn my flesh. "I have more money than I know what to do with, David. You need money—I need fun. We trade and we'll both be better off. Is it a deal?"

"A deal," I agreed, and patted the back of her hand. She tightened her fingers and wriggled closer so that her shoulder nudged me and her thigh lay warm and soft against my leg. I could even feel her garter clasp pressing into me.

"Have you eaten?" I wanted to know. When she shook her head I went on, "Then we're dining at a little place which serves the finest soft-shell crabs you ever bit into, and imported, unwatered French wines. The tab will come to around fifteen, twenty dollars. Fair enough?"

"David, please," she protested.

"All right. I'm sorry. But I want you to enjoy yourself and not wonder if maybe this is going to cost you a lot more than you figured."

Her answer was direct. She unclasped her pocketbook, opened a grained-leather wallet and took out all the folding money in it. "There's over five hundred there. It's all yours. Show me a good time tonight, that's all I ask. I don't want any of it back." She pushed the roll into my slacks pocket, down deep. Her fingertips were exciting as they moved around. When she sat back she had a smile on her face.

I swung off Collins Avenue and headed toward Carol City, about thirty minutes away. There was a bistro there, the Sea Chest, where I'd been known to come in the past and work at spending some of the allowance my father handed me every week. They knew me, liked me, and saw to it I got good service. I wondered if they'd learned I didn't have a penny to my name.

Bad news had traveled slowly for a change. The hostess gave me a toothy smile and an excellent table under some expertly draped netting in a dim corner. The candlelight made Mrs. Travis' face seem younger. She put her nyloned knees on either side of mine and squeezed.

"Thank you, David—for bringing me here, I mean. I like it. Already I'm having fun." I put my hand over hers and held it. Her smile told me she liked what I'd done.

I ordered a decorated concoction called a Manta Sting which was served in a bowl for two, with straws. It was a heady drink, made with rum, sherry and pineapple, and tasted like ambrosia. Mrs. Travis had to lean forward to sip from her straw and the blue organza obligingly fell away a second time. For a small woman her bosom was impressive. I cautioned her about sipping too fast. A Manta Sting is no drink to fool with, despite its smooth taste.

We dined on soft-shell crabs when the Manta Sting was gone. By this time Mrs. Travis was flushed and her knees were beginning to play games under the table. Not exactly impervious to the rum and sherry myself, I joined in the fun. The tables at the Sea Chest are intimate little arrangements. By putting a hand below the tablecloth, I found I could run my fingers up under her skirt and along her nyloned thigh as far as her garter clasp. It added to her excitement.

I decided on an orange pudding liberally sprinkled with almonds and wine for dessert. By the time my companion was done with it and the coffee royale, she was glowing. She hoped the evening would go on like this, so she could keep floating around on the nice pink cloud.

When we left the Sea Chest I walked her through the moonlight to look at the fish pond and its submarine lighting effects. I kept my arm about her waist until the cool

9

night air dissipated some of the fumes muddling her head. Then I took her to the Fleetwood.

She turned to me as I got in, expecting a kiss.

I kissed her slowly, with pleasure. It had been a long time since I'd kissed a woman—or a girl, either, for that matter. Three months, to be exact. When I learned I was getting none of the eighty to a hundred million my father wanted to leave me, the bottom dropped out of my world. And that included a few debutantes and married socialites with whom I'd carried on affairs of varying intimacy.

Her mouth was warm and wet, her tongue flavored with coffee royale and Manta Sting. When I bit it gently she moaned and rubbed her full bodice against me. Sliding my palm under her organza dress I moved it up past the garter clasp onto soft, smooth thigh flesh. I gripped her hard, then began stroking her skin.

"David, David," she gasped, head back and eyes closed. She was actually trembling. "It's been so long, so long. Oh, I haven't felt this way in years. In years. Every part of me is alive. I just can't get over the fact that I only met you a couple of hours ago."

I took away my hand and let her go back to normal breathing. The play was up to her, actually. She had paid out good money for an evening of togetherness and it was her right to call the shots. Right now I was hoping she wanted the same thing I did. Frankly, it had been a while since I'd felt so alive, myself.

She was sitting with her head on the seat back, eyes closed, her ripe mouth a little open. Her hands rested on her thighs, balled into tiny fists. Every so often they would jerk spasmodically.

"You wanted to go dancing," I reminded her.

"I know," she whispered. "I still do. Just give me a few minutes to pull myself together. Please?" Her eyes opened to study me. "How many women have you played escort to, David?"

I shook my head. "To none, for money."

My brutality made her wince. She sighed and looked down at her fists, slowly opening her fingers and working them together. "Miami Beach could be a gold mine for you. You know that, don't you?" It was her turn to be brutal.

Her slim fingers went to her black hair, faintly streaked with gray, pulling down the car mirror and switching on the courtesy lamp so that she might study herself in its

10

polished surface. Fingertips pushed and patted for a few seconds until she had her wave bouffant where she wanted it.

She smiled brightly. "I mean it, you know. Have you any idea how many women come down here to Florida during the winter season? The widows? The divorcees? I'm sure you do."

"In a vague way. I've never thought about it."

She looked at me steadily. "No, you haven't, have you? You're telling the truth, I can tell. Really, David, you're wasting your talents chauffeuring Continentals. You have a flair for this sort of thing—taking lonely women out and showing them a good time. I honestly mean it."

I let her lash out at me with words. Maybe she was flaying herself with them at the same time. There was no meanness in what she told me, no animosity; only a kind of surprise as if she'd struck pay dirt in a mountain stream.

"You give a woman the little attentions she loves. You order a meal with a deftness which tells her she'll enjoy it. Your eyes flatter her. Your hands go just so far, leaving it up to the woman herself as to how much farther she wants you to put them."

"I should say thanks, I suppose."

Her hand caught mine, squeezing the fingers. Concern made her face turn grave. "Oh, David—please don't misunderstand me. I love being with you. I do. I'm so happy we bumped into each other. You don't mind my talking like this, not really. Do you?"

I gave her a slow, friendly smile. "Not really."

Nor did I. I pride myself on being realist enough to accept the fact that two and two add up to four. What this woman was telling me was true enough—I did have a flair for the social graces. All my life I'd been practicing them as Randolph Mason Horne's only child. Never until tonight had I realized I might make money from them.

And I needed money. Oh, how I needed it.

Listening to her talk was bringing an idea to blossom inside my head. Earlier, she'd given me five hundred dollars. I would spend maybe fifty, sixty dollars of that on her. I could keep the rest. It beat babying Mark Continentals all the way from New York.

Rhoda Travis would be in Miami for the next week. If she was as prodigal with money every night as she'd been this evening, by the time she went back to Westport I ought to have myself a nice bankroll.

11

Earlier, I'd informed her I wasn't a gigolo. At the time I hadn't been a paid escort. Now, after becoming one, she was telling me how good I was at this game, how very much she enjoyed being with me, letting me show her the town. If I was that good, I ought to make it my business, I thought.

All my life I'd been to the most expensive resorts, backed by the Horne millions. I knew the right foods to order and what wines went with them. I could speak French fluently and was fairly conversant with Italian. I was young and strong, standing six feet one inch and weighing in the neighborhood of a hundred and seventy pounds. My blond hair was crew cut. I looked like an Ivy League college boy, the kind most women go for in a big way. I wore clothes as if they were a part of me.

These were my assets for this kind of business.

I was a natural for the game.

The fact that I might have a weak character never entered my head. I was merely taking the line of least resistance to the money I had to have if I wanted to go on living in the manner to which my adoptive father had accustomed me. An athlete sold his body to a baseball or a football team, just as a prizefighter did his to a promoter. Bright young men traded their bodies to business corporations in exchange for cash. I would be selling mine to women.

It was that simple. To me, it made sense.

I became aware that Rhoda had gone right on talking while my mind had wandered.

"You know how a woman feels when a young man treats her this way. It just melts her inside. She wants to be grateful. The only way she can show her gratitude is with money."

"Yes, of course—with money," I murmured.

"An older woman can't flatter herself that her charms alone will be payment enough for these services," she was saying slowly, staring straight ahead. The thought came to me that she was arguing with herself and had forgotten all about my being in the car. "She wants to be loved—yes, and to give love. But she has to tip the scales in her favor with hard cash."

"You make me sound like meat in a butcher shop."

She went on as if I hadn't said a word. "A lot of older women have money to burn. That's why you see so many of them down here in Florida. And they're lonely. Oh

God, are they lonely! Their husbands are dead or have left them. Sometimes they get so hard up for companionship they feel like climbing walls."

She glanced at me from the corners of her eyes. She knew I was with her, all right. "A man is different. He can pick up girls, pretty girls, in bars and such. An older woman is different. Too many men want the young stuff. The older you get, the tougher it is to wangle yourself a date—the kind of date you want to go out on, that is. Most any male will be happy to crawl between the sheets with you for a quickie, but I'm not talking about that.

"It's this other thing you have, this flair. You talked to me as an equal, not as if you were doing me a favor by being seen out in public with me. You took over completely. You made me feel as if I were your date, some fluffy young thing you were trying to impress. Oh, it wasn't put on. I mean, you weren't giving me an act. You were perfectly natural about it. A woman can tell.

"You didn't patronize me. You enjoyed my company. As a result, you gave me back my youth. You made me feel young and desirable."

I said in amusement, "This is quite a pitch you're giving me. You make me think I ought to make it my life's work."

"You could do worse, David. Do you know how many women there are in America who are single, divorced or widowed? Over twenty million. A lot of them are well heeled and willing to pay for services rendered. You have a ready-made market any time you want to have business cards printed."

" 'Have fun, will travel,' " I paraphrased.

"Something like that, yes," she commented wryly.

We sat in silence for a few minutes. I was thinking that maybe Rhoda Travis really had hold of something. Unwilling to handle a regular job—for one thing, the kind of job I could do wouldn't pay me the kind of money I needed—this other deal would be right up my alley. I wondered what she was thinking.

She told me, "Or maybe I'm just justifying myself, talking like this. I'm having such a good time, I can't believe it. I even feel guilty about it. Isn't that ridiculous? I'm trying to make myself better than I am by running you down. David, I'm sorry."

"For what? For telling the truth? You're perfectly right. I've been listening to you, agreeing with everything you've had to say. I'm not fitted to do any other work. I'm no engineer, no architect. I'm not even good at mathematics. Or at anything else which would earn me what I consider a decent salary. So why should you apologize?"

I kept my voice level, not showing anger or hurt. As a matter of fact, I wasn't quite sure whether I felt any emotion at all. Mrs. Travis stirred beside me, reaching out for my hand, bringing it between her palms.

"Why don't you hate me, David? I said unforgivable things just now. You're a very pleasant, handsome young man. Is it your fault you didn't inherit the millions you'd been led to believe you would?"

"No, I suppose not. Still, if there was good strong stuff in me I'd be working for the Horne Corporation. I've had it in the back of my mind to apply for some sort of job with Dad's holding company. I haven't so far because I've been afraid of the job they'd give me. Menial stuff, maybe. Bottom of the ladder and all that. I could take that if Dad were still alive—I'd know I would be moving up that ladder damn soon."

"I could get you a good job in New York," she said hesitantly, watching me carefully. "I have friends, connections."

"I might take you up on that," I told her, laughing.

"Oh, please do, David. It would be wonderful."

My eyebrows arched. "These friends of yours would like that, wouldn't they? You come back from Florida with a—shall we say, a protégé?—a young man who takes you out to dinner, to the theatre and night clubs. What would your Westport friends say about you then?"

"That would be my problem."

"And mine," I said, putting the key in the ignition slot. "I'll think about it, Rhoda. Maybe we could work something out."

She murmured plaintively, "I feel as if I've spoiled the evening. And I was enjoying myself so much."

"On the contrary. We've grown to know each other better. You aren't a stranger any more. You've become an individual."

Her smile was tight. "You even say the right things."

The big Fleetwood flowed through the parking lot and out onto the street. I drove mechanically. My mind was busy with other matters.

Finally I said, "Trouble is, you're fighting yourself. You want a good time but you don't think you should. It's an American attitude. Your Frenchman or Italian isn't both-

14

ered by puritanism. When he sets out to paint a town red he does it in spades, without fretting, without worry."

"You've been to Europe?"

"Half a dozen times—London, the Riviera, Capri, Venice with its canals—I spent three whole summers there during my college years."

We talked lightly, casually. Both of us were glad to get away from the past few minutes, which had left a bad taste in our mouths. Rhoda chattered on the way women will do while closing their minds to unpleasantness. I was her sounding board, letting her throw words at me and tossing them back at her. By the time we were on the Dixie Highway she was sitting over against me with her head on my shoulder.

"Where are we going, David?" she wondered suddenly.

"Little place I know. The Reef in Coral Gables."

"Do they have an orchestra?"

"A five-piece combo that vibrates."

"I haven't danced in such a long time."

"You leave everything to me, Rhoda. Don't worry about a thing. A man who knows how to lead properly can make any woman follow him."

"This I have to see," she cried and clapped her hands together. I glanced sideways. The laughter was back in her eyes and, for a while, she'd forgotten her guilt feelings.

To my pleasant surprise, she turned out to be a good dancer, with natural rhythm and graceful movements. Though she protested her lack of knowledge of the steps, I took her through a rhumba and then a cha-cha with such ease that when we were walking back to the table a couple of merrymakers applauded us.

"You're a miracle man," she sighed, sipping her rum and tonic. "An absolute twenty-two karat miracle man. I don't know what I'm doing out there but you make me go about it so easily, my feet perform without my even being aware of them."

"A man dances with his hands, too, you know. He must know how to guide his partner this way and that, turning her at the right moment, bringing her along with him."

The Reef serves good rum. One drink inevitably leads to a second and then a third. By that time you're way out, man, and eager for more. I had to stay sober, so I slacked off. Mrs. Travis drank as if it were going out of style. After her fifth, I told her she was coming apart at the seams.

Her earlier muscular co-ordination was gone. Rather

15

than follow my lead, she showed a tendency to cling. In a way, it added to her attractiveness, for her moving thighs came soft and warm against me, stirring me pleasantly. After a while we moved around the dance floor in a mist of Chanel and controlled desire.

At one o'clock I decided it was time to pick up the tab and say good night. I urged Rhoda out into the cool night air and the starlight, my arm about her middle. As we walked she caught my hand and lifted it up to her brassiere. I found her breast to be firm and heavy.

Twenty feet from the Fleetwood she turned to me, arms going around my neck as she mashed her lips on mine. "We've been teasing each other long enough," she breathed. "Come on, you handsome young bastard—kiss me."

We stood in the middle of the parking lot, highlighted by the full moon. I don't know whether anybody was looking at us but I kissed her the way she hungered to be kissed, listening to her whimper deep in her throat. Oh, I was a natural at this sort of thing, all right. I had her steaming before I turned and half carried her to the big Cadillac.

"You want to pick out the motel?" I asked when we were moving along the Coral Way. She was having hand trouble and breathing harshly.

"Hurry up. Just hurry up, David."

"Yeah," I agreed wryly. "I'd better do that."

I signed us in as husband and wife. I used my own name. Why not? I was single and without entanglements. I knew it was a misdemeanor in New York to sign a hotel or motel register with a false name; I wasn't sure about the Florida law, so I played it safe.

I closed and locked the door behind us. Mrs. Travis was lifting her blue organza dress as I switched on the electricity. Hidden bulbs made the bedroom bright as day, giving me a good look at her legs in blue nylons, her slightly tanned thighs and black girdle.

The dress was off. She tossed it on a chair and held out her arms. Above the black satin girdle she was wearing a brassiere, black with lace inserts to show the pallor of the firm flesh crowding its C cups. She was erotica in three dimensions, having pushed her guilt feeling away into some remote corner of her mind.

I caught her against me and began kissing her big red mouth. My lips moved to her throat, to her plump shoulders, to the quivering flesh of her upper breasts. My hands inched under the black girdle and gripped smooth, naked buttocks. I took my time, not hurrying, wanting her half out of her mind with need before I satisfied her.

In a little while she was absolutely helpless. She undressed me with shaking hands. She kissed my body, begging for my love, promising me money—all kinds of money —if only I'd do what she wanted so desperately to have me do.

After a while I gave myself to her.

We woke up twice during the night. The concealed lighting was still on and the bedcovers were down around the footboards. She was in her forties but her body was wildly alive, demanding, striving blindly and hungrily to make up for the long years of her widowhood. She lived seven empty years in five hours.

It was ten o'clock the next morning when we woke the third time. She stretched, arms high over her head. Then she lay there and let me look at her.

"Marry me, David," she said softly.

I shook my head but leaned over to kiss her. "I'm not the marrying kind, Rhoda. Besides, when you get back to Westport you don't want me around. This is your vacation. You're out to enjoy yourself. Don't get entangled in a way you'll be sorry for later on."

"I wouldn't be sorry."

"Yes, you would. Not right now, not for a year or even two years maybe, but eventually you would."

She considered that thoughtfully and nodded. "You may be right. You probably are." Rhoda swung her legs off the bed and padded, naked, her fleshy buttocks jiggling slightly, to where her black satin girdle lay wrapped around her blue nylons. Bending, she picked them up. Her buttocks were white and full. She came padding back to the bed and sat on its edge to undo garter clasps and unravel the stockings.

"Breakfast together?" I asked.

She turned her head to smile down at me brightly. "Of course. And after that a swim in the ocean. Then lunch together—wherever you say."

I grinned. "Aren't you wasting money at the Eden Roc? Why don't you just move in with me?"

Her eyes lighted up. "Would you mind, David?"

"I want you to. At least we can play at being married."

She leaned toward me, her big white breasts swinging

17

outward to rest on my chest as she kissed me. I stroked her naked back. When she began to breathe faster I dragged her down on the rumpled sheets. I told myself my customer might as well get her money's worth . . .

We ate pancakes smeared with maple syrup, and drank hot coffee at a sweet shoppe. I drove Rhoda to the Eden Roc and waited while she packed her things, then brought her to the parking lot where I'd left my Alfa-Romeo.

Now that I had a bankroll I could fill my convertible with oil and gas. I picked up a picnic basket and a thermos at a drugstore. There are some lonely spots on Key Biscayne where a man and a woman can laze around in the Miami sun. I figured that if we liked it enough, we wouldn't have to come back to the motel until after dark.

I loaded the wicker hamper with sandwiches and hard-boiled eggs. I filled the thermos with coffee. When I showed Rhoda what I'd done she clapped her hands like a little girl.

"I feel as if I were going on a date, the way I used to back in Westport before I got married," she said with a pleased laugh.

"Well, you are going on a date," I said.

To my amazement she blushed and ran into the bathroom to change into her swimsuit, a Tiktiner bikini with cardigan to match, made of stretch nylon. It clung to her with indecent honesty. She'd never have dared wear it at a public beach.

I slipped into my trunks while she checked the picnic lunch. I put on a beach jacket with pockets to hold the car keys and my wallet. I decided to use the Alfa-Romeo. It would be unfamiliar to her and would add a sense of newness.

I took the Rickenbacker Causeway to Key Biscayne.

The day was perfect for the beach. The sun was hot but the air was dry and pleasant. Rhoda bubbled with laughter, with carefree merriment. Bare legs stretched out as much as the Alfa would allow, she prattled on about her Westport neighbors, its country club, her golf game, and how she hated to think of going back.

I hunted a more or less private strip of beach. When I found it I carried the hamper and the thermos, a beach blanket and two bottles of suntan lotion. All Rhoda had to burden herself with was her transistor radio.

We lay in the sun for hours, listening to music. Alone

like this, Rhoda could let down her halter while I rubbed Coppertone on her back. Lying on her front, she got a good tan from her shoulders to her middle. After a while she fell asleep.

I did a little dozing myself. What with one thing and another I hadn't had too much rest the night before. When I wasn't sleeping, I was planning. Everything was working out just right for me. I figured that if I was going into this escort business, I'd better learn all about it. Rhoda Travis liked to sun-bathe. Maybe she'd like to play a little golf tomorrow. My membership dues at the Miami Country Club were paid up, thanks to my father. The day after that, we might charter a boat and run out into the Gulf Stream. The main thing was, keep the customer happy.

My next client might like horse racing. For her there would be Hialeah Park at the end of N.W. 79th Street. Or if she wanted to get in some shopping, the Lincoln Road stores were waiting. My tactics called for a visit to a number of places to see what sort of deal I might work out. After all, if I brought in business I was entitled to a cut of the profits.

It was almost dark when she stirred, rolling over on her back, an arm flung across her eyes. Her breasts were big and white, with thick brown nipples, soft now and relaxed, but they could get hard and swollen with passion. One thing I had to remember, I told myself: these widows and divorcees came to Miami for a good time. If what they were after included some bed calisthenics, that would be a part of my trade, too.

With Rhoda Travis, it had been easy.

There would be others, though, who might be difficult to take. I'd seen enough lonely women during the traveling years with my adoptive father to recognize the signs when they came up flashing. Fat women, thin women, pretty women and plain, all kinds came to the vacation resorts, and a lot of them had a gnawing hunger. If I contracted to slake those hungers, I'd have to live up to my bargain.

"David! Why didn't you tell me?"

She was sitting up, lifting the striped halter to cover herself, glancing at me sideways. I grinned and winked. "The scenery was too good to spoil."

Rhoda was like any other woman; she enjoyed flattery. I could see her hiding a smile even as she chided me. When the halter was in place I poured the rest of the coffee in a cup and handed it to her.

19

"To warm you up," I explained.

Over the paper rim her eyes regarded me. "What's on the program for tonight? The Sea Chest again?"

"Not twice in a row, love. We go stepping this evening. A gown for you, a dinner jacket for me."

"Ooooh, it sounds like fun. Where?"

"You'll see." I grinned and, getting to my feet, helped her up. I did the menial work, folding the blanket, repacking the hamper. Rhoda Travis was on her vacation. I wanted her to know it every minute we were together.

She held my hand, walking back to the car. That night, for the first time, she would tell me about Felicia Marr.

TWO

WE WERE CLINGING in a dreamy waltz at the Cloud Nine under a glass roof so clean it seemed we were in the open air. The stars were high above, music was all around us, and we were joined about as closely as two people can get without being ejected from a night club.

"Felicia would love this," she murmured.

"Oh?" I breathed into· her perfumed hair. "Who's Felicia?"

"A friend of mine. A career girl—woman, rather. Worth even more than I am. Felicia Marr. Married three times, divorced three times. Right now she's a bundle of neuroses."

"Recommend me," I said casually.

She pulled away so she could look up into my face. I noticed she still clung to my body with her hips and thighs, working them smoothly in the dance rhythms. Under her silver lamé evening gown she was stark naked except for an ornate garter belt and gunmetal nylons. I knew because I had watched her get dressed. She was soft and exciting. In a rather sly way we had been making love even while we danced.

"I intend to recommend you, David," she said seriously. "Felicia needs relaxation. She owns three or four big corporations. They keep her always on the go. I don't know when she's taken a day off."

"Talk her into coming down here. I'll show her around."

She put her head back on my chest and let me understand how hard her breasts had become. "Just the sights, David," she whispered. "Not the other. You know . . . like this." Her hips moved where they pressed into me. "Or your motel room. Please? Not that."

"Certainly not," I said.

"You're laughing at me," she said without glancing up. "I guess I can't blame you. If Felicia decides she wants you, she'll get you. She always gets what she wants."

"Always?"

"Always. Without fail."

"She sounds dangerous."

"Sometimes I think she is. But maybe I'm worrying without reason. Bram Skoronski will probably be with her."

"The current boy friend?"

"He's a little more serious than just a boy friend. He wants to marry her. Felicia's a proud woman. It bothers her no end that she's made a mess of her three marriages. She doesn't want another fiasco."

"This Bram boy feels he can make her happy?"

"He does. Except that he's dark and probably thirty pounds heavier, he's something like you—casual, sophisticated, knows his way around no matter where he goes. The Copa, an ocean liner, a dive in Harlem, Bram always fits right in. Before you know it he's talking with the boss, ordering drinks for everybody within hailing distance and generally taking over."

The music stopped. With a hand on her bare elbow I guided Rhoda back toward our table. Her lamé gown picked up reflections from the candles and wall sconces so that it seemed she was bathed in light. At that instant I considered her the most attractive woman I'd ever known. I told her so as I held her chair so she could slip into it.

"Wait'll you meet Felicia," she said.

"She begins to intrigue me, this Felicia Marr."

"I've known her since we were schoolmates at Bryn Mawr. The Gordons—she was a Gordon before her first marriage—and my own family became friends through our acquaintance. I was her maid of honor when she got married. Two years after she married Fred Ostringer, she went to Reno."

She accepted one of my Old Golds, bent for the light. The lamé gown clung more closely than had the blue organza. In one way, it was a good thing—she wore no brassiere under the evening dress.

"I will always wonder what happened between her and Fred. They seemed made for each other. They liked the same sports, golf and swimming, enjoyed playing bridge as partners—which is a recommendation in itself—and had the same tastes in theater and in music. They lived in a

21

seventeen-room mansion in Scarsdale where they entertained lavishly every other weekend. Fred was with International Telephone. Still is. He made enough money. I know that wasn't the reason for the break-up. Maybe it was because Felicia wouldn't give up her business career."

"Smart girl, was she?"

"Incredible. Went into the Gordon Enterprises when she came out of Bryn Mawr. In five years she doubled its size. Her father often told me he could retire and that Felicia would run his holding corporation better than he did. Toward the end she did just that—before her father died from a heart attack, I mean."

The music began again, a lively cha-cha, but we sat there, Rhoda Travis talking and I listening. "She was thirty when her father passed away, and she'd been married a year and a half. Right after that, her marriage began to go to pieces. She stood it for six months, then packed her bags and got her divorce. Fred didn't fight it. You'll see them together occasionally even now, over a bridge table as partners—I said they played well together, didn't I?— or maybe in aisle seats at some theater or in Carnegie Hall. They're still good friends. Fred remarried, some blond thing ten or twelve years younger than he is. They have two children."

"And Felicia?"

Her ringed finger crushed out the filter end of the cigarette, rubbing it around and around on the glass ash tray. "She married two months after Fred did—it was almost as if she'd been waiting for him to make the first move—a French count named Gui Philippe Simon de la Carere. He was older than she by fifteen years, and had a reputation for being a daredevil. His sport was racing cars. He used to enter the Le Mans run every year, for a while. He came in second on one occasion.

"Felicia changed all that. They spent their honeymoon at the Riveria, sun-bathing and swimming. Later, she told me Gui was as restless as a caged animal just in from the wilds. They lived in Paris for a few months. Gui's business was publishing and his offices were off the Champs Elysées.

"I never did learn what went wrong. One day I got a letter with a Paris postmark, saying she was radiantly happy. Three mornings later she rang my front doorbell— she and Gui were finished. She went to Reno again. Gui didn't contest the action. Next spring, driving a Maserati and trying to overtake Juan Fangio in the Grand Prix of Monaco, he went into a log barrier. For a little while Felicia was inconsolable, blaming herself for his death. She used to say they could have made a go of it if she hadn't been so headstrong. She never explained what she meant and, frankly, I didn't have the nerve to ask."

I signaled the waiter for refills. Tonight Rhoda was drinking daiquiris. She went on dreamily, as if looking directly into the past. "Felicia was all business after that— for the next five or six years—devoting herself to Gordon Enterprises. Things began to boom in the early Fifties and she rode the crest of the wave. Her holding corporation diversified its interests. Its stock went up over a hundred. She sold her common shares for a tremendous profit but stayed on as president. Two years ago she bought it back around twenty. She owns it all now."

"Quite a gal," I said, because I felt Rhoda expected it. "Oh yes, quite a girl. And desperately unhappy. Now me, I enjoy my wealth. I spend it having a good time. Not Felicia. She hoards it and spends sleepless nights thinking up ways to triple it. Sometimes I think she treats a dollar bill like a lover."

She sipped the daiquiri. "Her third marriage was the funny one."

"In what way?"

"He was an artist, a big hairy bull of a man. Felicia had become interested in some off-Broadway theater group, putting up money for productions, even going so far as to have her own accountants try to put it on a paying basis. I believe she flirted with the idea of invading Broadway with her young talents. Instead, she got interested in the man who painted the scenery, Cletus Marr."

Her eyes swung back from across the room where she had been staring. She smiled apologetically. "I thought I recognized someone. No matter. Where was I? Oh, yes— Cletus. He was as strong as an ox and hairy as a bear. He adored Felicia. I understand he's a good journeyman artist; no genius like Picasso or Kokoschka but good enough to earn himself a nice living with the right connections. Felicia saw to it that he made them.

"Advertising stuff, mainly, with a mural here and there for a clubroom or a school. He got top prices—Felicia saw to that, you can bet. Every weekend she went down to Greenwich Village where he had a dinky room and stayed with him until Sunday night, posing for him, feeding him thick steaks and good whiskey, and, I suppose letting him make love to her. Felicia is full of nervous energy. One way for her to get rid of some of it is by going to bed with a man. Anyhow, he was her bull and she was his heifer. Everything was idyllic for a time."

She raised her hands to her temples and rubbed them. In the candlelight, her face looked taut, strained. I put my hand on her wrist. She opened her eyes and smiled wearily.

"Too much sun this afternoon, I think," she murmured.

"Headache?"

She nodded and closed her eyes.

"All right, home we go." I stood and caught up her mink stole. She protested that it was only a little past midnight and that the evening was still young, but she rose to her feet and let me drape her smooth white shoulders with the fur.

I ordered a container of tomato juice with an egg broken in it as I paid the bill. I carried the package out to the car. On the way back to the motel I stopped off and bought ice from a vending machine.

Rhoda lay with her head back all the way home. When I braked the car, I saw that she was asleep. I got out of the car, unlocked our motel-room door, then went back and lifted her in my arms. She muttered drowsily about being able to walk but I shushed her with a kiss and carried her to the bed.

I added rye to the egg and tomato juice, shook it up with some ice and made her drink it. Then I eased her out of the lamé gown, the garter belt and stockings, and tossed her evening pumps under the bed. I pulled the covers over her and turned out the light.

In five minutes she was asleep.

I was too restless to sleep. My mind kept running over what she had told me about Felicia Marr and her three husbands. She sounded like a typical rich bitch—neurotic and domineering. A woman who played life the same way a man did, hungry for power and for control. What she could get no other way, she bought.

I wondered about the hairy artist, Cletus Marr.

Felicia had married him, I knew. So far in her life story of the amazing Felicia, Rhoda had not covered their wedding—or their divorce. She still used his name as her own. For all I knew, maybe she still spent her weekends in his atelier, feeding him steaks and whiskey.

I smoked two more Old Golds right down to their filters. My Accutron said it was two o'clock. I got out of my clothes and slid between the sheets, next to Rhoda. It was after three when I finally dozed off, to dream of a twelve-foot-tall Felicia Marr clad in leopard skins and with a long bullwhip which she cracked with snaps like rolling thunder as she drove herds of men ahead of her, harnessed to a gigantic chariot. I woke in a cold sweat. They had been leading me toward the traces, and the bullwhip had come scorching down my shoulders.

Rhoda slid over toward me during the night. I put my arm around her, pulled her close. She was a normal, aging woman, filled with the usual worries about her lost youth. In a way, I was intensely fond of her.

I wished she hadn't known Felicia Marr, though.

Maybe I was just being psychic.

We chartered a motor launch that afternoon, an Owens Sea Skiff which could bunk four people. It glistened whitely in the sun, cradled on the smooth waters of Biscayne Bay. Rhoda fell in love with it right from the start. Nothing would satisfy her but a shopping trip along Lincoln Road for boating clothes.

"Oh, please, David. Please? May we go out for a couple of days, just the two of us? Can you run a boat well enough to make it safe?"

"I used to own a Chris-Craft Constellation. Actually, it was Dad's boat but I ran it from the time I was twelve."

"Oh, David. I'm so excited!"

She went a little wild on Lincoln Road, insisting on buying me some yacht clothes and a cap with plenty of brass all over its peak. Then she abandoned me to spend four or five hours loading up with tapered pants and middies, cover-ups and jackets. I spent the time buying food and liquor. If she wanted to get away from it all for a few days, I didn't intend starving to death.

We got under way before six, after a quick supper at the Chez Bon Bon. The sun was low on the horizon, its redness glinting in a path of scarlet along the bay waters. The motor purred smoothly, sweetly; the rental company took good care of its craft. Rhoda was sitting up on the foredeck, skirts to her hips, unfastening garters and rolling down her stockings, laughing like a little girl.

"I'm going to go barefoot all the time," she called to me. "No more shoes, no more stockings."

"Your feet'll spread," I yelled back.

She stuck out her tongue, reached under her skirt and yanked down her garter belt. "I'm free," she caroled. "No more girdle, no more belt. Just your girl friend in her pelt."

"Ouch," I said.

"May I, David? Go around in my pelt on the boat?"

"Sure, just so long as no other boat heaves in sight."

"You'll warn me, won't you?"

"I'll warn you," I promised. I didn't want her pulled in for indecent exposure. The coastal waters were off limits to nudists.

She came down the sidedeck on light feet and stepped on the coaming, then to the floorboards. Putting her arms around me, she kissed me hungrily. I hugged her tight. She was soft, warm, exciting with only herself under her dress. She'd taken everything else off up on the foredeck.

"Hungry?" she wanted to know.

"In every way."

Her nose wrinkled at me. "Where's the kitchen?"

"The galley is forward."

"So's the guy steering the boat," she giggled, writhing her backside away from my pinching fingers.

"They call the kitchen a galley on board ship. And forward means up ahead. Behind is aft."

"Leave my aft alone then, skipper—or I'll never cook your meal. And I feel domestic."

I watched her fanny waggle down through the companionway and toward the little cookstove and tiny refrigerator that comprised the galley. Then I had to use my eyes on the markers up ahead that showed the channel. I could hear pots and pans clattering and pretty soon I caught the smell of frying ham, potatoes and scrambled eggs.

I felt good—real good. I hadn't been this way since my adoptive father died. The feeling came to me that I was beginning a new way of life with Rhoda Travis. Maybe it wasn't what I'd have done if I had a choice, but at least I was able to do things I liked, taking a boat through the coastal waters of Florida, with salt spray in my face and dying sunlight warm on my skin.

We ate on a little table in the cockpit, talking together as if we'd known one another all our lives. Rhoda stopped laughing once to give me a peculiar look.

"You have a rare quality, David," she murmured slowly. "You can make a person forget herself. It would appeal to Felicia Marr."

"You have a complex about her."

She shook her head. "She used to be an awfully close friend. Then—oh, I don't know—we grew apart. I think she's unhappy—desperately unhappy. Maybe her nerves are too tense or she's overtired. Anyhow, this sort of thing would be good for her."

"Can she cook?" I taunted with a grin.

Rhoda stuck out her tongue, then leaned back on the cushioned transom seat and stretched. "I feel absolutely newborn. Like a little child."

I lit two cigarettes and passed one across the table to her. "Tell me the rest of her story. You left off where she and this artist boy, Marr, were having a ball for themselves, with her posing and him making money doing commercial art."

She drew a deep breath on the cigarette and let smoke swirl out her thin, aristocratic nostrils. "They got married, of course about eight, nine months after they met. Don't ask me why. It wasn't Felicia's doing. After her first two marriage failures I think she got a complex about wedding rings.

"Maybe Marr insisted. Despite his bohemianism, there was a streak of honest Iowan manhood deep inside him. He was from the corn belt, incidentally. Claimed to have won any number of husking bees at state fairs."

"They didn't hit it off," I guessed, "because he wanted to go back to the farm and she was a city girl."

"On the contrary, Felicia loves the country. She bought a big place up in Connecticut as a wedding present for Cletus, couple of hundred acres or even more, a place where he could grow pigs and cows and all the corn he wanted. It was within an hour and a half's drive to New York, so Felicia probably thought it was part of the suburbs. Incidentally, she lives there now. Cletus went back to Iowa after the divorce. She had one of the barns renovated into an artist's studio for him. She uses it now as an office. It's just the same way Cletus left it, with his sketches and half-done oils still resting here and there. Felicia had a big desk moved in, a filing cabinet and a desk for her secretary—Dori Pierce, her name is—and over long summer weekends she works there."

Rhoda stared off across the water, her eyes dreamy. It was nearly dark so I got up and turned on the riding lamps. The air had been changing while we'd been eating. It was warm now, moist and almost uncomfortable.

I got out of my T-shirt and poured Rhoda and myself some cold tea.

"The divorce," I hinted, sipping.

"Oh, that. Well, nobody knows for sure exactly what happened between Cletus and Felicia. He claims she tried to murder him. She slapped his face and had a good cry for herself, then went off to Reno."

"Murder?" I said. "A little drastic, isn't it?"

"There was an oilstove explosion in the studio. It damn near got Cletus. The funny thing was, if Felicia hadn't come down with a headache that morning and begged off from posing, she and not Cletus would have been there when the stove blew up.

"It was her custom when she posed for him—always at ten o'clock of a Saturday morning—to go alone to the studio-barn and get into whatever outfit she was to wear while posing. Cletus always joined her later—say, quarter after ten or so. This morning I'm speaking of, Felicia had her headache so Cletus went alone to the studio, to put away his things. It was then that the stove exploded."

"Didn't she point this out to Cletus?"

"Certainly. He claimed she only pretended to have the headache. It was she who told him to go to the studio and straighten up his things. She was going to drive to a nearby lake to swim. She wanted him with her."

"But—my God, you don't accuse your wife of trying to kill you because there's been an accident."

"Oh, she and Cletus had been tiffing off and on for a week or two. Felicia can be rather trying when she isn't getting her own way. It was about one of Cletus' former models, some girl or other Felicia didn't like. A redhead named Eve. Seems Eve had a chance to get a good job— not in modeling, in fashion design, which is what she specialized in at school. She could get it if Felicia would recommend her. Cletus asked her to do it, as a favor. Felicia blew her stack. Accused him of carrying on with Eve behind her back. Utterly refused to recommend her for anything but a house of prostitution, or words to that effect.

"Cletus got mad and walked out. He went to see a good friend of Felicia's, a big wheel with one of the New York department stores. The man said he'd recommend Eve on Cletus's say-so.

"Naturally, when Felicia heard that, she threw a tantrum—called Cletus a few choice words, telephoned the department store bigwig about Eve, but he'd already sent in his letter recommending the girl. Oh, it was a fine few days, believe me.

"I guess Felicia remembered her other busted marriages because, after a while, she calmed down. Tried to patch things up. She was going to pose for Cletus as a peace offering. Then the stove went up.

"Seems Felicia had made some threats against her husband which Cletus remembered. He thought she'd rigged the stove to go off, maybe just to scare him. Felicia went to Reno. End of third marriage. Period. Finish."

The night was warm, blue velvet wrapped around us, with the stars and a three-quarter moon peeping down. The water was silver fire all around the hull. We sat awhile, just thinking. At least I was thinking, wondering whether or not I wanted to meet this Felicia Marr.

Rhoda brought me back to the moment by standing and lifting her left arm, the better to run down the zipper on the side of her dress. "Any law against moonlight swimming, Davey?" She was bending, lifting the dress hem over her tanned thighs to the pallid flesh of her hips, then upward over her head. She wriggled getting it past her hair, making her full breasts do a little jump and bounce.

I was right. She didn't have anything on under the silk serge sheath. Her plucked eyebrows arched. "Well, darling? Any law?"

"None at all. Wait a sec and I'll join you."

She stepped to the stern deck and was overboard before I could slide out of my slacks. Inside of ten seconds I was diving myself, going deep, enjoying the feel of the water on my skin. She was treading water when I surfaced.

"It's glorious, simply glorious," she said, her face lifted to the sky. "I've never done this before—swimming bare-ass, that is. I love it."

"The only way," I agreed and caught hold of her, drawing her close. The feel of her wet, slick skin pressing against me was wildly exciting. Her heavy breasts rubbed back and forth on my chest as she twisted to free herself, laughing delightedly, and the brush of her smooth thighs against my loins built a fire in my blood.

"David," she breathed harshly, clinging. "Oh, David."

We kissed and caressed one another there in the water, breathless with excitement. There was a smoothness about her flesh which was new and different. As far as we knew we were the only living things in these immediate coastal

29

waters. Overhead the stars stretched for light years on all sides, like a cosmic canopy. It was almost as if we were the only man and the only woman in the world.

Her hair was wet and heavy, falling to her shoulders, all its careful curling gone. Without make-up, and stark-naked, she was like a primeval woman. Whatever inhibitions she had left after our few days together she'd tossed overboard when she jumped from the stern. She used her hands and her mouth on my body as I was doing with her, panting harshly, fitfully, whispering that she loved me, adored me, that she wanted me always for her own and would kill anyone who tried to take me from her.

"Hey, relax," I said. "What's this talk of killing?"

She strained into me, eyes dark and feverish in the night. "I will, David. I swear to God I'll kill her if she takes you from me the way she takes men from everybody. I mean it."

"Sure," I said, "but let's not think about that now."

She was on the verge of hysteria with what I was doing to her and her bleak thoughts of Felicia Marr. I didn't want a hysterical woman on my hands, so I began swimming toward the boat, tugging her with me. I helped her up the little ladder, kissing the backs of her heavy thighs as she mounted the treads.

Rhoda Travis was waiting for me when I came over the rail, hands reaching out to clasp and fondle, her voice a deep purr of pleasure. Pulling me to her, she wrapped wet arms about my shoulders.

"What about the bunk, honey?"

"No, David. No. I can't wait. Please. Here."

"Right like this? In full view of anybody who cares to look?"

"Let them look. I don't care."

"Not even if I do this to you?"

She panted harshly, quivering, head back, teeth sunk into her full lower lip. "Yes—do that. Oh, God—yes!"

I turned her a little so that she tottered on shaking legs. Oddly enough, even while I was kissing her, I was thinking that Rhoda Travis ought to be good for a couple of hundred dollars tip when she said good-bye to me. If this was work, I loved it.

She was clawing me by this time, sobbing uncontrollably. I let her do what she wanted, in sympathy with the terrible need that was all but shaking her apart. I wondered if Felicia Marr ever let herself go like this with a man.

From what Rhoda had told me about her, I'd bet against it. To me, she sounded like a conceited, selfish bitch.

"David, David, David," Rhoda moaned.

I folded my arms around her, drew her against me. There was no time for either of us to find the bunk now. It had to be here under the night sky with the air cool on our damp flesh, clinging and whispering and rocking together in a bursting nimbus of white flame and ecstasy.

We spent four days on the Sea Skiff.

Most of the time, neither of us wore any clothes. We were out of sight of land, and whenever a passing boat came into view we slipped into our swimsuits. Rhoda got her tan. All over. So did I.

We never mentioned Felicia Marr again, not until we were heading homeward, the salt waters of Biscayne Bay foaming under the keel. It had been an interlude of sun and wind and water, a time for doing whatever we wanted to do, with no man-made laws to keep us in check, no voice to cry halt or hand to gesture a halt to our actions.

She had brought her Swiss Hassekblad camera with her and insisted on taking my picture dozens of times, gripping the helm, raising the anchor, with and without my swimsuit.

"Nobody'll make those prints for you," I told her.

"I'll make them myself. My husband was a bug on amateur photography. He taught me how to develop negatives. I have a darkroom at home."

"You'd better keep a couple of those pictures under lock and key. There are laws, you know."

She wrinkled her nose at me. "When I get tired and bored I'll take them out and look at them. Who knows? Maybe the sight of them will make me realize what an idiot I am to stay up north when all I have to do to see you is hop a plane for Miami."

"Just don't show them to Felicia Marr."

I meant it as a joke, but she refused to laugh. Her plucked brows gathered in a frown. "I'm sorry I ever mentioned her to you."

"Oh, come on. I was only fooling."

"She destroys everything and everyone she touches. There's something about her; I don't know what it is or how to explain it. She has such tremendous personal charm and yet—"

She broke off to brood, staring out over the water.

"Why'd you mention her at all if you hate her so much?"

"I don't hate her. I rather like her. She's a friend of mine—a good friend, I suppose you might say." She smiled brightly as if forcing herself. "It's just that I've fallen in love with you, David. It's stupid of me—I didn't mean to do it. At first you were just a handsome youngster, someone to play with. I knew you could show her a good time, which is why I told you about her.

"Now I don't want her to so much as see you. I'm afraid for you. Oh, I know, female temperament and all that. I'm being utterly silly, I realize. If she ever got her claws in you, something awful would happen."

"I'll clip her claws," I threatened, grinning.

"Not you. You don't have the strength."

We left it like that, with me faintly hurt and Rhoda almost tearful because she'd been so unthinking. She decided she had to kiss and pet me into a good humor, which she did by the time we were docking at the marina, making me feel like a petulant child.

This was to be our last night together.

"Tomorrow I have to fly home, David," she told me as I tooled the Alfa-Romeo up Collins Avenue. "I wish I could stay longer but I simply can't."

"We'll make it a night to remember. Cocktails and dinner at the Americana, then an evening of drinks and dancing at the Carillon."

Flushing slightly, staring straight ahead at the imposing bulk of the Fontainebleau, she murmured, "We won't stay too long at the Carillon, will we? I—I need a good night's rest for the trip home."

"Just two drinks and four dances. I promise."

I held to my word. At midnight we were back in the motel room, but not to rest. I gave Rhoda Travis a final night which would keep her warm with memory all during the winter. She fell asleep with exhaustion as the sun was coming up over the Atlantic.

I drove her to Opalocka Airport next morning.

She kissed me good-bye, tears in her eyes, assuring me that when I got tired of Miami all I had to do was look her up and I had a job in her dead husband's concern. The offer of marriage still went, too. But I knew I was a better playboy than I'd be a husband.

I waited until the plane was a dot in the sky. Then I went back to my motel room. I had seen Rhoda putting an envelope in the new valise she'd bought me as a going-away present and my fingers itched to open it.

There was a thousand dollars in the envelope, in crisp, new twenty-dollar bills. A bonus for good behavior. All together, Rhoda Travis had been good for two thousand, four or five hundred dollars, what with gifts and incidental money she'd slipped me from time to time. It beat driving Mark Continentals to Florida markets, that was for sure.

I had found the job that suited me.

THREE

I TOOK A VACATION for the next few days, lazing around on the white sands of Key Biscayne during the sunlight hours, and taking in a few movies at night. I wrote to my Harvard classmate, telling him I wouldn't be playing chauffeur any more, that I'd landed a job in Miami. At the same time I dropped a few lines to Rhoda Travis, letting her know I missed her, which was true, and that I had something lined up here in Miami which would keep me on the straight and narrow, which was a boldfaced lie.

When I began eying the girls on the beaches in their tight Jantzens and Helancas, I decided to hunt up another customer. I found her in a little bar just off Bird Boulevard, looking as lonesome as a lost child and nursing a daiquiri.

She was expensively dressed in a tight, black cocktail sheath. The diamonds on her fingers and about her wrist were real. Her legs in tight gray nylons were still good. Maybe her hips were inclined to spread a little but her breasts stood out big and firm.

"May I?" I asked, snapping a lighter for her cigarette while she was fumbling in a big leather handbag for matches. Her eyes came up, startled and grateful, to stare into mine.

"Why, yes—thank you," she said breathlessly.

At first I thought I'd made a mistake. She didn't open up and gush the way most lonely women do when you make a play for them. And unless I read the signs all wrong, she'd been sitting here at the bar waiting for just such a play.

Now she seemed reserved, almost shy.

The thought came to me that she wanted to play but was too fearful. A lot of women are like that, living a

33

secret kind of life deep in their own minds but desperately afraid to put their thoughts into action. I gave her time to get used to the idea before I moved in.

When she ordered another drink, I said lightly, "You'll spoil your appetite for dinner."

Her eyes looked at me for the first time since that original hurried glance. "It doesn't matter," she said softly. "I'm not hungry anyhow."

"Then you've never tasted *mole pablano* at the Crystal Grille."

"No, I never have. Is it so good?"

"Look, they know me there. Why not let me scribble an introduction so you and your husband can try it some night?"

"I—my husband—that is, I'm alone."

She was divorced, Helen Ewing told me over her third daiquiri—eight months ago in Chicago. Her husband had left her for another woman; it had been a terrible blow to her pride, to her womanhood, I gathered from the tone of her voice. She was getting good alimony and she had money in her own name. She was in Florida trying to forget her ruined marriage—and not doing a very good job of it.

I invited her to eat *mole pablano* at the Crystal Grille. She hesitated, looking shy again, but I had my fingers under her elbow and was guiding her off the bar stool and toward the front door before she could gather her wits. I figured what this one needed was a firm hand.

She was laughing breathlessly but happily as she got into the Alfa-Romeo. I took time out to light a cigarette for both of us before turning the ignition switch. Once she had taken the plunge, she was keen for the idea of being picked up by a young man half her age.

On the way she said hesitantly, "Please, you must let me pay for the dinner. I'm so grateful to you for suggesting it—oh, I'm going about this all wrong. What I mean is—"

I saved her further embarrassment by admitting that I was out of a job temporarily. "I found myself with two hundred dollars in the savings bank and no prospects of any more money coming in," I lied casually. "I blew it all coming down here."

She was instantly sympathetic, and insisted on slipping three twenties into my jacket pocket. To cover gasoline, she added. I looked at her when she said that, but she'd meant no sarcasm. She was just good-hearted. I wondered about her husband.

She loved *mole pablano* and the white wine I ordered with it. We danced twice. She was not a good dancer but she was easy to lead. I had her doing steps she never dreamed of, before the dessert was served.

Quite chastely, I returned her to the Eden Roc before midnight.

"I will see you again, won't I?" she asked.

"First thing tomorrow morning, if you say so. There's a quiet little beach I know where you can sun-bathe in complete privacy. I have enough left from that sixty dollars you gave me to fix a picnic lunch."

Her handbag was open instantly. She shook her head when I protested, opening her wallet and taking out some more twenties, pressing them into my palm.

"Please, David. I have plenty of money, more than I know what to do with. I won't have you spending what little money you have left. Please take it. As a favor?"

I took the twenties, slipping them into my own wallet.

When I got back to my motel room, the telephone rang. It was Rhoda Travis, her voice faint with distance. She sounded excited.

"David? Darling? It's Rhoda. Are you surprised?"

"Of course I am. How are you?"

We talked about how much we missed each other, then she came to the point. "It's Felicia. I ran into her yesterday in town, at Lindy's. Before I knew what I was doing I was telling her all about you."

"How'd that happen?"

"I said what a marvelous time I'd had and mentioned a couple of places where we'd been together and when she said I sounded like a Miami native—well, I admitted to meeting a simply fascinating young man who'd been kind enough to show me around the better places and—"

She ran on for a while, torn between regret at having let Felicia Marr know about me and pride in having had a young lover for herself.

"She said she might be going to Miami Beach soon, if only to lay eyes on you. David? You won't let her do more than that? Just let her look at and talk to you?"

"Cross my heart and hope to die, I won't."

"I just had to call and tell you, I was so angry at myself. You can't imagine the names I called me all the way home."

We chatted for a little longer before we blew kisses at each other and she hung up. Talking to Rhoda made me remember our nights together and the four days in the Sea Skiff. As I put on my pajamas I wondered if Helen Ewing liked boats.

She was waiting for me on the sidewalk next morning as I slid the Alfa-Romeo in against the curb, attractive in harlequin sunglasses and a black cotton cover-up with peppermint-striped bows running down its front. Her legs were pale but agreeable to look at between the hem of the cover-up and her cork beach-clogs. I assumed she was wearing a bathing suit because, at first glance, she seemed stark-naked under the black affair she was sporting.

"I'll get absolutely blistered," she told me, settling beside me in the bucket seat.

"I have a beach umbrella. And a bottle of lotion."

"Do you always think of people's comfort this way?"

"Only when they're pretty girls."

She gave her breathless little laugh and stretched out her fine legs. I figured it was time to get more personal than I'd been the night before so I put my hand on her somewhat heavy thigh as I drove, touching it lightly.

"You have very fair skin. I don't think I'll let you cook too long. Maybe an hour, hour and a half. No more."

When she didn't pull away from my palm, I knew I had her. She wanted attention and affection, just as Rhoda Travis had wanted it. She was afraid, though. Well, I knew the answer to that problem.

I played beachboy with the umbrella, the picnic basket, the suntan lotion and blankets, just as I had with my first client. Helen Ewing ate it up.

I was spreading a blanket on the sand of Key Biscayne when she slipped out of her black cover-up. She was wearing the scantiest damned bikini I'd ever seen outside the French Riviera where they wear something they call *le minimum*. The halter just about covered her nipples. The pantie part began four inches below her navel and ended high on her thighs.

"Is it—too skimpy?" she asked, flushing.

My smile told her I liked her in it. "Out here we're away from people—and policemen. This is a holiday and when you're on a holiday you do whatever you want to do."

"I never thought I'd wear it, not really. I can't imagine what made me buy it in the first place."

"You need a good figure to wear it," I said "You have a

good figure." And she did, except for a little too much width to her hips. Her breasts were big but they only sagged slightly in their full maturity.

My hand indicated the beach blanket. "Lie down so I can get some of this suntan oil on you."

She lay down and cushioned her cheek on her crossed arms while I filled my cupped palm with Coppertone and began spreading it across her back. Except for a thin black band where her halter tied, and that tiny strip of bikini pantie, she was absolutely naked. There was plenty of soft, white flesh to absorb the lotion and I took my time spreading it on.

She was purring by the time I told her to roll over on her back. Her arms stayed where they were, covering her face, while my hand and the suntan oil went over her legs and exposed midriff—to cover her blushes, maybe. She was soft and fleshy and felt good under my fingers.

With my hands just below the beginning swells of her breasts I said lightly, "You can take your halter off here, if you want. There isn't anyone around—but me, that is. And I won't look if you don't want me to."

She drew a deep breath so her breasts almost came out into the open by themselves. Her crossed forearms came down and she looked at me. There was a livid heat in her eyes and I told myself it was these quiet ones you had to watch out for when they kicked free of the traces.

"Yes, I'd like that. You take it off for me and rub some oil into me there. And David. Watch what you're doing."

I did what she told me. Her naked breasts were hard and swollen as they came out of the halter. I oiled them slowly, gently. The thick brown nipples jutted upward into my palms all the time I was coating them with lotion. Her eyes were closed but her red mouth was open as I went over those big white breasts until they glistened. Her hips were squirming into the blanket before my hands finished with her.

"Now the panties," she whispered.

"Uh-uh," I told her, turning her hip so I could slap an exposed buttocks where her bikini bottom had pulled back. "I can't take any more of that, lover doll."

"You can't leave me like this," she panted. "I haven't had any man except my husband, not ever. With him it was always a kind of chore, something I had to get over and done with. Like this—with you—I've never been this way before."

37

"We'll go back to my motel room early."

She came up on an elbow, reaching out a hand and running it up and down my thigh. "You promise, David? You really mean it?"

I told her I meant what I said and that I was just as anxious as she was to relieve her need. I made her lie back and bake in the sun.

"For an hour. Then we'll go swimming."

I put up the beach umbrella so she could lie under it after going in the water. All the time she watched me, running her eyes over my body. She held my hand when we went in the surf and clung to me below the surface. I had to pry her loose when it came time to eat.

Helen Ewing was no longer reserved or shy. She sat close in the Alfa-Romeo, all the way back to the motel, and from time to time she would turn her head and take a slow, gentle bite of my shoulder.

"Five hundred dollars," she said once.

"What?"

"Five hundred dollars," she said more clearly. "It's all yours, David. If you treat me good in your room."

"I'll make you cry uncle for that kind of money."

"I don't know the word," she smiled.

"You will, you will."

I took a shower with her, getting rid of the sand and the suntan oil on both our bodies. My soapy hands running over her nakedness was an exquisite torture, she told me.

I was toweling her dry when the telephone rang.

I think I knew, even as I stood with the water dripping off my naked body, who was at the other end of the line. The voice was low, husky. I knew who it was right away.

Felicia Marr.

When she spoke my name I felt the tingle right down to my toes. She had a way of getting through to a man right away, without preliminaries.

"Where are you?"

"Still at the airport. I telegraphed ahead for reservations for myself—and for you—at the Fontainebleau."

"For me?"

"Darling, you don't think I came down to Miami Beach to go slumming in some little motel, did you? How soon can you meet me?"

Helen Ewing came out of the bathroom and walked across the thick wall-to-wall carpeting. She put a knee on the edge of the bed and smiled at me.

"I'm busy tonight," I said to Felicia Marr.

Delighted laughter tinkled in my eardrum. "Darling, you're incredible. Is she right there? Now? All set for some bed calisthenics? Oh, you're priceless. Rhoda was right about you. I admit candidly I was a little dubious about you. But you see, I know Rhoda so well, and since I can read her like a book I knew no ordinary boy could put those stars in her eyes—"

"I'm sorry," I cut in. I can't possibly see you before tomorrow."

"Five thousand dollars, David."

"Wha—what?"

"I said I'll give you five thousand dollars to drop whatever it is you're about to do and hotfoot it over to the airport right now."

"Don't be ridiculous!"

"Ten thousand, darling. Just to come and see me. Let me think—your motel is off the Palmetto Expressway. I'll give you fifteen minutes to dress, ten more to get here. You have a car. Allow five minutes for possible traffic tie-ups. Within half an hour, if you walk through the airport doors, I'll put my personal check for ten thousand dollars in your hands."

There was a click.

I stared down at the receiver, my heart thudding wildly. Ten thousand dollars, just to go see a woman named Felicia Marr. I didn't have to take her out or make love to her or anything else.

Helen Ewing was lying on the bed, looking at me. "Who was it? Some woman?"

I nodded. "She just offered me ten thousand bucks to meet her at the airport in half an hour."

"You're kidding," she said, sitting up.

"I think I am, too, but it's what the lady said."

I reached for my shorts where they were hanging over a chair back. Helen Ewing let out a wail and scrambled off the bed.

"David, you aren't going? After what you promised?"

"I'll be back. I just want to earn myself some money."

"I won't be here," she threatened.

I grabbed her and kissed her mouth hungrily. "You'll be here. We'll go out and wrap ourselves around the best filet mignon Miami Beach can serve up—after we spend a few hours making love, that is."

Her face was drawn as she stared up at me. "You won't

come back. I know you won't. All she'll have to do is offer you more money and you'll stay with her. For however long and for whatever reason she wants to keep you with her, you'll stay."

"Honey, I swear by all that's holy. Give me one measly hour to go there and come back. Just one hour."

She looked little and tragic, standing naked on the carpet, while I got into my tropical slacks and sport shirt. She seemed suddenly older, tired. Faint lines crept down from her nostrils and gathered at the corners of her mouth. The breasts that had stood up so proudly at the beach and in the shower, drooped noticeably. Even her belly appeared to pouch.

"I was afraid to hurt your feelings by offering you money," she said brokenly. She walked toward her clothing, dispirited and dejected.

"Helen, wait," I exclaimed, catching her arm. "Please, just give me an hour. I'll be back. I swear I will."

"You poor bastard," she said tonelessly.

"Felicia Marr doesn't mean a thing to me. She's just a rich woman who throws her weight around. I've never even met her."

Her eyes were steady, probing into mine. She paid no attention to her nudity, as if aware that it could never again stir me, never hold me against the tug of ten thousand dollars. It did not matter now whether I saw her without her clothes; I was no more to her than a piece of furniture.

"Go ahead and sell yourself to her, if you want. It's your life. Maybe once she gets her claws in you, you'll look back on this night and wish to hell you hadn't run off and left me. Oh, God! I feel so ashamed of myself. So ashamed."

She dropped onto the edge of the bed and wept bitterly into her cupped hands. I looked down at her, then at the door, then at my wrist watch. A little more than eleven minutes had gone by. I had less than twenty minutes left in which to get to Opalocka Airport.

"Helen, just wait for me. Hell, it isn't the end of the world, you know. Any time a guy can make that much money by driving to an airport, he goes and earns it. You know anybody who wouldn't?"

She made no answer. I opened my hands and closed them tight, wanting to grab her and shake some sense into her head.

"Please, Helen. Wait for me. I'll be back inside of an

40

hour. I swear it. Look, I have to run if I'm going to make it on time. But wait." I opened the door and stood for a moment, staring back at her. I said once more, "Wait an hour. See if I'm not back."

She just went on crying into her hands.

Traffic was light along Okeechobie Road. I made good time. There was six minutes to spare of my half-hour when I walked into the airport waiting room and ran my eyes around the people waiting there.

I knew her right away.

She was smaller than I imagined, very dainty in white sharkskin with a matching toque on her black hair. There was an elfin quality to the face she turned toward me as I approached and a funny little smile played around the corners of her pouting lips.

"David," she cried softly, making a caress of the word, and came to her feet with her hands stretched out, standing on tiptoes as if to make herself taller.

I took her hands in mine and worked up a smile. An imp of laughter lay deep in her purple eyes. "You're even better-looking than I'd supposed," she said gently.

I had to be cruel. "The money?"

She stared at me, then bit her lip, nodding. "Yes, of course. I have it right here." She opened her handbag, lifted out a small checkbook and tore off the topmost check. It was made out to me and was signed by Felicia Marr.

When the check was in my hands, I folded it carefully and put it in my wallet. I was very conscious of her nearness and of the extremely faint perfume that lurked in the folds of her clothing. I told myself to swing around on a heel and move off. Helen Ewing might still be waiting in my motel room; I owed her a damned good steak for what I'd done.

"I had it all made out," she said in a small voice. "The check, I mean."

"You were pretty sure I'd come running," I muttered.

She nodded gravely, her purple eyes steady on my face. "I knew from Rhoda you weren't a fool. Only a fool would turn down that much money just to travel a dozen blocks and let a woman look at him."

"Or a man with pride."

Her hand lifted to her forehead in a tired gesture. "Don't fight with me. Please? I'm too exhausted to fight.

41

You can go now. I've seen you. You've earned your money."

She stood there waiting, regarding me with that intent stare as if she were probing deep down inside me and learning what made me tick. I shuffled my feet. I had time to drop her off at the Fontainbleau and still get back to the motel within the hour limit I'd set for myself.

"My car's outside. May I drop you anywhere?" I asked.

"Oh, would you? I'm afraid I'm rather a bad girl. I sneaked off by myself—left everyone home—they're probably wild by now, wondering what happened to me. Marta—she's my maid, been with me for years—Doctor Vance, Gerard, all the others. I really have to phone them. Would you mind waiting?"

I thought about Helen Ewing. "Can't you telephone from the hotel? A half-hour isn't going to make much difference."

Her eyes widened. "Of course I could. Why didn't I think of it? Here," she added as she turned, "I have a bag somewhere." I saw a small valise of genuine cowhide and bent to pick it up. It was brand new, with the sheen still on the leather.

"Is this all?" I asked.

She giggled like a little girl. "Isn't it awful? I made up my mind so quickly I didn't have time to do more than send out a girl from the office to buy a few things and a bag to put them in. I came right from work, you know—took a taxi to the airport. It was a spur-of-the-moment thing."

She must have been forty if she was a contemporary of Rhoda Travis, but she was so slim, so small of bone, that she seemed much younger. Her thick black hair showed not a single gray strand under the waiting-room lights. Her middle was slim, almost flat, but it was the aliveness inside her that made you think of youth. There were moments when Felicia Marr seemed to bubble as she walked along beside me on quick, darting feet.

When we came to the big entry doors she caught my free arm and hugged it to her in an excess of gaiety while her laughter rang out. "I haven't had a vacation in half a dozen years. Not a real vacation. Just weekends—a holiday here and there. Now I'm in Miami Beach."

I grinned down at her. I couldn't help it. The *élan vite* in her tiny body was a magnetic force which made you react to it.

From the corners of her eyes she caught my expression and spread her hands at me. "I've never been in Miami Beach before. It's all new and different." She let her eyes wander as she walked where I led.

She squealed when she saw my white Alfa-Romeo. "It's darling. And it goes with you, David. It goes very well." Her purple eyes stared from me to the car and back again. "You know, I had you tabbed as an MG type. I don't know why. But now I see you and your car together. You fit so well—your blond hair, the crew cut, your strong young body . . . tall . . . wide shoulders . . ."

"You're embarrassing me," I lied. I enjoyed every word with which she praised me and wanted more.

I opened the car door and made a little bow and a gesture of my hand. I will never know why. A psychiatrist might tell me it was a symbolic thing, that by bowing to her I was in effect surrendering to her loveliness, her spirit of aliveness. Maybe. Or maybe she made me think of the French Riviera and the blue grotto of Capri and unconsciously I adopted continental manners, where it is fashionable to bow to a lovely woman and kiss her fingers.

I put the cowhide valise in the trunk, then climbed into the driver's seat. There is an intimacy about an Alfa-Romeo, as if its sides gather closer around you when you are inside it, pushing you and a girl together. I felt it strongly as I drove toward Collins Avenue and the Fontainebleau.

Felicia Marr said, "Rhoda was right, you know."

"Oh? About what?"

"She's been telling me I need a vacation."

"This is the place to have it."

"Oh, yes. It's all so wonderful—like a whole new world. There must be so many things to see, so many places to go. And the sun—the big, hot, wonderful sun baking you to a golden brown. Mmmmm."

She wriggled deeper into the cushion, closing her eyes and leaning her head back against the top of the seat. I ran my eyes down her body, seeing the large mounds of her mature breasts, the faint arch of belly and the width of almost girlish hips. The sharkskin skirt hid her thighs but below its hem, pulled up an inch or so above the knees, her legs were slim and nicely curved.

Could this woman really be Felicia Marr, the Felicia Marr whom Rhoda Travis had made out to be, in my mind at least, something of a rich, spoiled bitch of a society

43

woman who had caused the death of one husband, the near-death of another? She had been married and divorced three times. Everything she touched, human or inanimate, she broke or ruined.

I made a sound in my throat. Impossible!

If I didn't know how old she was, I'd have thought her to be my own age. A young girl setting out on a date with her boy friend, no more. Not an industrial tycoon, certainly, with millions of dollars always at her fingertips. A younger married woman, maybe but not a divorcee three times over and maybe itching to take herself another husband.

Suddenly I had to know more about Felicia Marr.

With my own eyes I needed to study her, to make my own judgment. I would depend on Rhoda Travis no longer. If she was the tyrant rumor made her out to be, she would betray herself. All I had to do was give her the opportunity and watch.

"You must be starved," I said.

"Mmm, I could eat."

I drove past the Collins Avenue turnoff and continued on along the North-South Expressway. "I know a place, the Seminole, where the rum drinks are like nectar and the charcoal broiled steaks melt in your mouth."

"Sounds like a slice of paradise."

She had turned her head so her left cheek rested on the seat back. There was a wistful smile on her face and her eyes were big and hungry. Her hand came up to touch my hand where it gripped the wheel, pressing it gently.

"I like you, David," she said softly. "Very much."

Then she took her hand away, but I rode through the last few hours of the dying day with a kind of inner glow. I felt like a rich man bestowing alms, for some stupid reason. I told myself I was nuts.

Helen Ewing might be waiting for me in my motel room, yet here I was driving this divorce to the Seminole and feeling good about it. I knew what she was; Rhoda Travis had told me clearly enough; if I had the sense God gave little chipmunks I'd push her out at the next street corner and run for my life.

I kept on driving and feeling good about it all.

Every man creates the seed of his own destruction.

The Seminole was rigged out in Indian fashion, with polished wooden poles to represent the beams and thatched roofs of a typical home in a Seminole village. The tables and chairs were carved in a lifelike imitation of outdoor furniture. The waitresses wore authentic Seminole garments, even to the blue beads at their throats. The headwaiter was dressed as Osceola himself might have been, years ago. A mock tomahawk was thrust into his belt.

Felicia Marr loved it.

She ate ravenously, without apology for her hunger. She drank three rum collinses, almost without pausing. Always her eyes sparkled with delight and her voice went on bubbling with pleasure. In nervous reflex her hand would come out to touch mine, to run gentle fingertips over my skin, as if they were absorbing some force my body was giving off.

Then she would pull away her hand and look embarrassed.

I got the feeling, after a while, that there was something about me she needed very badly. My youth, maybe. Or my enjoyment of the things that have to do with the senses. It is a nice feeling to be wanted, to be needed, even if you don't quite understand why or how.

I wondered if Helen Ewing was still waiting.

In the glow of the small table lamp, nothing seemed to matter except this gamine of a woman sitting across from me, her purple eyes studying me so wistfully, her lovely face tender and vulnerable. I found myself waiting for her quick smile which seemed to include me in her happiness, for the quick brush of her fingers.

Neither of us was dressed to enter the Cloud Nine or the American Bar of the Eden Roc, so I took her dancing at a dimly lighted bar and grille near the Rickenbacker Causeway. She could dance like an Arthur Murray instructress. We floated around the floor as if we were on a cloud. The cha-cha, the waltz, the fox trot, the rhumba—we did them all. Perfectly. Felicia Marr had feet of quicksilver. There were no steps too complicated for her to follow.

"We could make a living at this," I told her.

She moved lazily against me. "Mmm. Don't talk."

Her eyes were closed. She was lost in a puff of contentment, moving easily and without effort. I got the feeling that a part of her had gone off and left the whole world behind, that she ran barefoot through the sand of some mental Nirvana, shrieking with joy. I wondered if I was with her in her dreams.

When the music ended, she whispered, "Take me away now. Put me to bed so I can go on dreaming and not wake up for a long, long time." Her eyes were still closed and the wisp of a smile was printed on her mouth.

She had to open her eyes to walk to the Alfa-Romeo but she shut them again as she sank into the seat and kept them that way all the way to the Fontainebleau. I know because I was looking at her face when I didn't have to watch the traffic.

As I braked the car, she murmured, "Your room is right next to mine. Go into the lobby and wait for me. I'll register."

"You're kidding."

"No. Please. I have everything planned."

"But my things are in my motel room. I can't walk into this place in slacks and a sport shirt and—"

There was no question in my mind that I would refuse. It was just that I was unprepared.

"I have a surprise for you, David. Don't spoil it for me. Everything is going just right for me—thanks to you, darling David. So please? Please?"

The little-girl quality was in her voice. I shrugged, got out of the car, walked around it, and opened the door. She put her hand in mine, let me help her out.

We walked into the huge lobby side by side. Obedient to her wishes, I went to the chair and sat down to wait. There were men and women in evening clothes on all sides of me. They stared at my slacks and sport shirt. I thought about the ten-thousand-dollar check in my wallet and told them, mentally, to go to hell.

She was at my side almost immediately. "Everything's taken care of, darling. Come along now."

For one breathless moment I felt a terrible, insane fear clutching at my guts. All at once our roles seemed to have been reversed. I was not the dominant personality any longer. It was not David Mason Horne who was taking care of Felicia Marr but Felicia Marr who was taking care of me.

There was an emptiness in my middle as I stared up into those suddenly cold, hard, purple eyes. They were living amethysts in her lovely face, almost hypnotic in their effect on me. I had become nerveless all of a sudden.

I told myself I was a damned fool.

The evening showed a ten-thousand-dollar profit, so far. Maybe the next few days with this woman would double

46

that, which wasn't bad for a young guy just going into business for himself. I got out of the chair and walked after her and the bellhop.

Like a dog trained to heel.

In the elevator we stood close together. Her face showed no emotion whatsoever. I must have been imagining the hardness in her eyes, down in the lobby. When the elevator stopped, we got out.

The bellhop opened her door and flicked on the lamps. It was a big room, done all in white and gold. Then he turned and brought me to the next door, opened it and went in to hit the wall switch.

I followed him in, feeling sheepish. The boy was too well mannered to smirk or look wise. He had his livelihood to make, too. My hand went into my pocket, peeled off a five-dollar bill and handed it to him.

"Thank you, sir. Thank *you*."

He moved across the room to a little alcove and opened the door there. It gave onto a combined bath and dressing room. "It connects with the room next door, sir," the boy told me.

It was my turn to say thanks.

The bellhop went out and closed the door behind him. I wandered around the room, studying the ornate furniture, the thick carpets extending from wall to wall. When my adoptive father had been alive I had become used to suites like this. It was a good feeling to be in one of them again. It was almost like coming home.

I walked into the bedroom.

I stopped and stared, not quite believing my eyes. All my belongings—everything I had left in my motel room a few hours ago—were here in the bedroom of the Hotel Fontainebleau. Even the new transistor radio I'd treated myself to yesterday morning had been brought over. It was as if Felicia Marr had taken possession of them.

My clothes, my shoes, my shaving kit. Everything.

Even me.

FOUR

FROM BEHIND ME I heard a door open.

The thick carpeting must have muffled the sound of her high-heeled shoes because when I turned Felicia Marr was standing in the bedroom doorway smiling at me. There was something bright and metallic in her hand.

47

"You found everything, I see."

I was beyond protest. "How did you do it? Why?"

"Money can do anything, darling. I simply phoned the hotel, told them to send two men to your motel room and bring back whatever they found." Her purple eyes laughed at me. "Evidently your lady friend was gone when they got there."

Helen Ewing. I'd forgotten about her.

She said, crossing to the clothes closet and sliding back the door, "For all intents and purposes, you're my secretary. That's how I registered you down below." With her left hand she caught the hanger that held my hundred-dollar sports jacket. Her right hand came up and now I saw what she held in it: a sharp knife.

With a single motion of her arm she drove the knife into the sports jacket. Three times she used it, making long slashes. She dropped the jacket on the carpet and reached for my Appia slacks.

"For God's sake!" I yelled. "What the hell are you doing?"

"Destroying your things," she said calmly.

The knife went into the slacks, utterly ruining them. There was no anger on her face, no emotion whatsoever, as far as I could tell. The knife did its slashing, savage work, and in five minutes every garment I possessed—outside of what I had on—lay in tatters at her feet.

"The valise," she said. "Put it on the bed and open it."

I did what she asked and stepped back. My shirts, my ties, my underwear, all felt the cold kiss of the steel. When they were shredded, she picked up my transistor radio, glanced at the trademark, and smashed it on the edge of the night table. She made me give her my silver cigarette lighter, my key ring and my wallet. She waited while I took out my driving license, a membership card or two, the check she'd given me earlier and the fifty-odd dollars I had left from squiring her to the Seminole and the bistro.

"I'll have everything thrown out within the hour," she said amiably, as if she were discussing the weather. "Now take your clothes off."

She was insane, but I did what she asked. I stripped in front of her, feeling those purple eyes crawling all over me. When I was down to my shorts I watched her use the knife on everything I had been wearing.

She held out her hand. "Those too, darling. The shorts, I mean. Hurry up. I've had a long day. I'm tired."

She stared at me as the shorts came off. For the first time I saw emotion touch her face. She went on looking at me even while her knife tore into my shorts.

"The shoes, too," she said softly. "And the socks."

Those she threw into the valise. Then she smiled brightly and said, "You don't have anything left, do you?"

"Only my car."

Her hand made a sudden little gesture. "I intend to sell that in the morning. I'll need the keys and the registration. Let me have them."

"You're mad," I said.

"I'm very sane. I'm just indulging myself, as I do quite often. The keys, darling. And the license. Please. Oh, yes. And the cash you have, except for my check."

"My God," I muttered and let her take them.

Her eyes went over me slowly. "Now all you have is yourself, David. Just you and the check I gave you."

"This is how you get your kicks?"

Her eyes widened. "Oh, no. Don't get me wrong." *Don't get her wrong, she says!* "I like you very much. So much that I'm going to own you. You had forty-seven cents when you met Rhoda Travis. You don't have a single thing now, except what I gave you.

"Tomorrow morning we'll go shopping, you and I. I'll buy everything you need from now on. Anything you want. Do you understand?" She came so close I felt the brush of her skirt on my thighs, the gentle pressure of her hard breasts under her dress and brassiere. "Tell me what you want and it's all yours.

"A Bentley Continental, perhaps, instead of the Alfa? Or a Ferrari? And better clothes than what you've been wearing. I told you I liked you. I do. Anything I like that much I have to own—all to myself. There must be nothing of anyone else about you. From now on you'll take your gifts from me."

Her soft palm touched my chest, ran down across my side to my hip. It burned like fire. There was a similar fire in her purple eyes.

"Just you, David—in your fine, brown pelt. I'm going to dress you from the skin out in the finest clothes money can buy."

"Like a toy, a plaything," I said dully.

"Something like that, yes. Oh, but it will be a fine life you'll lead—living in the finest hotels, eating the finest foods. Do you want a yacht? Rhoda told me you know boats. A Chris-Craft Constellation? A Matthews forty-two?"

"No. Nothing."

Her black eyebrows arched mockingly. "No? I think you will, darling. In time." Her hand caught the back of my neck, brought my mouth to her open lips. She kissed me, pressing herself against me. After a while she let me go.

"If I weren't so tired I'd stay with you, dear. But I'm not as young as I used to be. I need my beauty sleep."

Her hand slapped my flank. She laughed huskily and, without a backward glance, walked out of my bedroom into her own room. I heard the door close behind her.

I stood there, feeling lost and bewildered.

What in the name of God had I gotten into? Felicia Marr was a madwoman—or so terribly sane and powerful it was almost the same thing. I had wanted the good things of life that money could buy. Well, now I had them. Anything I wanted, she would buy me. Except my freedom.

I felt very cold, suddenly.

And frightened.

FIVE

I SLEPT WELL that night—like a baby.

In the morning when I woke, Felicia Marr was standing beside the bed in a black gauze nightgown. Her eyes were feverish as they studied me, but it was not her eyes that interested me at the moment. She was naked under the dark chiffon, and for the first time I saw her body. It was a good body—slim, with big breasts, and nipples the size of half dollars—formed with a gentle mound of belly and wide hips. Her thighs were ripely fleshed, her legs long and shapely.

As I say, I had slept well. I was feeling healthy. The woman standing beside my bed had given me ten thousand dollars the night before; even more important, she was very close, perfumed and available. I put my arms around her hips and drew her onto the bed with me. If I'd been more wideawake, I'd have noticed the quick tensing of her muscles, her indrawn breath and startled frown.

I bent over and kissed her, moving my hands under the transparent lace bodice, letting my fingers slide on her breasts. They were firm but getting soft—she was in her

50

forties, I remembered suddenly—but they were warm and exciting. I slipped a shoulder strap off an upper arm.

Her hand cracked hard against my cheek.

"What the hell's the idea?" I asked, startled.

Her smile was cold. "The idea is quite simple, lover boy. You belong to me. You move when and where I say. When I want to make love, we make love. Not before."

The little voice in my head told me to get out. I heard it but I paid it no attention. I was thinking of the check for ten thousand dollars on the dresser. Her face was inches below my own and it was curiously white, indignant and coldly angry, but my body was shoved hard against her black nightgown and she herself was just as naked under that as I was; her body told me it was having trouble obeying the commands of her mind.

"Sure, hon," I whispered softly. "You bet." I kissed her chin. "I just didn't know the ground rules, is all." Her hips moved almost imperceptibly where I pressed against them and I knew then that she wanted me. She'd had a good sleep and was feeling healthy, too. I added. "Forgive me?"

Her eyes flickered as I moved on her a little, getting ready to roll off. She said stiffly, "I forgive you. You—you couldn't be expected to know me and my ways—so early in our relationship."

I sat on the edge of the bed as she got back on her feet. She looked at me and her tongue touched her lips. She drew a deep breath as if something was hurting her. "We're going shopping this morning," she informed me.

"Do I go like this?"

She never took her eyes away. "Of course not. I've ordered some clothes sent up from a men's shop. They ought to be here any minute. I'll go get dressed."

I let her get almost to the door before I went after her. I caught her by an arm and swung her around, jamming her into me and holding her that way with my arms banded about her softness. I kissed her mouth, hard. I let her understand just how much I wanted the body she was showing off so effectively under the black nightgown.

Her arms came up to fasten around my shoulders. She slumped to me and her lips came open. A whimper grew in her throat. Those soft wide hips lifted and moved—against her will, I'm sure—and my skin felt the bite of her long red fingernails.

I let her go so suddenly she blinked in momentary dismay. Her hand came up again. She liked to slap, this one.

She hit me hard with her palm, jerking my head with the blow so that my ears rang.

"You bastard," she hissed, but her voice broke.

She turned and ran into her room, leaving me staring at the white paneling of the door she'd slammed in my face. I grinned. I was beginning to understand Felicia Marr. She had to dominate the male in her love-making. She had to be the boss. When she gave an order, a man jumped—or else. She stood for no nonsense, no independence.

She was frightened.

Of herself? Of the emotions that lay just beneath her surface? Did she fear that by letting herself submit to a man she would lose her individuality? There are women like that; I'd read about them in the psycho books. Felicia Marr was a study in the psychology of psychodynamics.

I went to the dresser and picked up the check.

I memorized it while my blood cooled.

We went shopping in the chic shops along Lincoln Road. I wore the pearl-gray slacks and sport shirt that had been delivered to my room within ten minutes after Felicia had left me. Surprisingly enough, they were a good fit. I supposed she'd gotten my measurements from the garments she'd had so much fun destroying the night before.

Money was no object with her. She insisted on getting me three of everything—slacks, sports jackets, shoes and loafers, underwear, shirts, a summer formal, street suits, cuff links and tie tacks. You name it and she bought it. The total bill came to somewhere between one and two thousand dollars. She only bought the best, the most expensive, as if anything cheap were somehow dirty and not to be touched.

Only once was there any embarrassment.

I was standing before one of those three-way mirrors in a Madras sports jacket and charcoal-gray slacks when the clerk turned to her with a broad smile.

"Your son could model for a living," he said.

She was sitting with her head tilted on one side, frowning thoughtfully, studying me. Her stockinged leg had been swinging back and forth. When the clerk spoke the leg forgot to move. She froze all over. Only for an instant, though. The leg began to swing again as she nodded pertly to me.

"I think that combination will do nicely, darling."

52

Her eyes talked at me across the space between us. There was hurt bewilderment in them and a plea for a denial of the words the clerk had said. Maybe when I get older and am trying for a little while to regain my lost youth, I will understand and sympathize with what was stabbing deep into Felicia Marr at that moment. But I was young and heedless of age, with no sympathy for, nor understanding of, its problems. I turned back to the mirror and studied the fit of the Madras jacket across my left shoulder.

In the glass I saw her biting her lip.

The moment passed—as all things pass away after a while. She put the cold veneer back on her face and took my arm when we left the store, chattering about Hialeah and how we must visit it at least once while we were here.

In another store a clerk thought we were newlyweds and that made her feel better. She laughed delightedly and hugged my arm; but later, while she was writing out a check to cover her purchases, I surprised a knowing grin on the clerk's face. I was honestly glad Felicia didn't see him.

She wanted to get some sun, so after Lincoln Road we went back to the hotel and put on our swimsuits. Her maillot-styled suit was a bouclé stripe affair, tight to the body and cut extremely low in the back. She had the body to set it off. She drew a lot of stares as we walked to the big pool.

We swam for half an hour, then relaxed on lounge chairs. I offered to coat her with lotion but she gave a faint shake of her head. I shrugged. If she wanted to burn, let her.

She only tanned, I discovered. Something about the texture of her skin kept it from going red. It became a golden shade that made her even more attractive. We stayed four hours in the hot sunlight, skipping lunch.

When she was gathering up her beach robe and handbag, I asked her if she wanted to go out to eat. I suggested the Desert Inn, then the Hideout.

"Just the hotel tonight," she smiled. "My first day in the sun always makes me sleepy. I'm going to bed early so we can have a full day tomorrow."

"Oh."

"A good night's sleep won't hurt you either, David."

"I'll catch up on my reading."

Apparently my sarcasm was too lightly applied. I could

have told her I was young and eager to go, that my idea of a good time wasn't sitting in a bed or on a hotel lounge reading a book, no matter how interesting. I saved that for the resting times between women. Instead, I went after her like a dog trained to command.

I lay awake in my expensive silk pajamas for a long time that night, staring at the ceiling, hands clasped behind my head, wondering about Felicia Marr. She insisted on taking the play away from me and into her own hands. I was not so much the hired guide and escort with her as I was the paid companion, always at her beck, her whim. I had no choice of activities. I went where she said, and acted as she wanted me to act.

Maybe I ought to have felt used, cheap. I did, but the thought of the ten thousand dollars I had put in the savings bank that morning—between visits to the Lincoln Road shops and while Felicia was picking out the maillot bathing suit—salved my pride. I could afford to feel cheap, I thought.

She had slipped two fifties into my hand for spending money, too—in case I needed cigarettes or a package of gum, she'd told me with a smile.

Kept man. Oh, well.

Where today, boss lady?

I had that thought as I tapped on the door between our rooms next morning. First there would be breakfast to keep up my strength, though why I needed strength for this sort of life I honestly didn't know. I felt like a work horse after three months on clover. And after a breakfast of ham and eggs and coffee I would get my orders.

"Come in," she caroled.

I opened the door and started to close it in almost the same motion. She was sitting at her vanity wearing a black lace brassiere, no more. She turned when I said, "Ooops, excuse me. I'll be back." She laughed at my expression.

"Silly boy. Come in, come in. Don't stand on ceremony."

I let my eyes touch her rumpled bed, the Jackson Pollock prints on the walls, the heavy brocade drapes, anywhere so I would not have to see her body. I felt she was laughing at me. Out of the corner of my eye I could see enough of her to know she had not moved. She was still half turned toward me, the hairbrush with which she was attending her mane of thick black hair suspended in a hand.

"David, look at me," she said suddenly.

"I'd rather not."

Her laughter tinkled. "Am I that exciting?"

Any woman would be that exciting, I wanted to tell her. I was too smart to go killing geese that laid golden eggs, so I whistled softly, put my hands in my pockets, and went to stand before a picture, my back toward her.

"You're priceless, angel—absolutely," she squealed.

She got to her feet and came across the carpet. She had high-heeled shoes on—besides the bra—I could hear them tapping as she came up behind me and put her arms around me, pressing her breasts into my back.

"Precious David," she murmured, hugging me. "Am I terrible to tease you so? I wish I could look into your head and find out what you really think about me behind that handsome face of yours."

"I just don't understand you," I said.

Her cheek rubbed my sport-shirt sleeve. I could see her glossy black hair and smell expensive perfume. "Poor darling David, I'm such a trial to him. He's never run into a woman like me. But I know what I'm doing, dear. Believe me."

"You're a sadist."

"Mmmmm . . . maybe. But for a reason."

"What reason, for God's sake?"

"You'll find out."

She hugged me once more and turned away to dress. I never moved. I stared at Pollock's *Masqued Image* until my eyes wearied. When the red and greens and blacks blurred together, Felicia was at my elbow, fully dressed.

"You can relax, sweetikins," she said dryly.

The simple shantung clung to her slim body. She looked chic and young, and only a close observer would see the faint lines at the corners of her eyes. It cost money for a woman her age to be so youthful. Only the ablest masseurs and beauticians had the ability to turn back the years in her flesh, to erase the troubles, the bad memories, from her face.

I began to earn my keep. I made a little bow and said, "You're lovely. I'll enjoy breakfasting across the table from you."

Pleased surprise swam in her eyes. "David, how sweet!"

She wanted to go to the races, she told me over breakfast in the main dining room. Somebody in New York had given her a tip on the Fifth, a horse named Futility. She

55

would give me the money. I would place the bet. A thousand dollars for her, a hundred for me. To win. Futility was a long shot, playing seven to two.

We walked out into the sunlight to the oval gardens fronting the Indian Creek yacht basin. She walked ahead of me, fumbling in her purse. My eyes were caught and held by a flaming red Oldsmobile Starfire sports convertible. I bumped into her when she stopped beside it.

Her hand came out of the purse holding a set of car keys. She dimpled a smile at me. "Instead of the Alfa, precious."

I swallowed hard as my fingers closed over the key ring. My hand went to the door and opened it so she could slide in on one of the bucket seats. Felicia was prattling as she settled herself, pulling her skirt to her knees.

"I wanted a Bugatti but I couldn't get one on such short notice—and we do need something to run around in."

I looked at her to see if she was needling me. She was honestly sincere. Money, to Felicia Marr, was a means to an end; the end being gratification of her whims. I told myself I was very happy to be one of her whims. It was a good feeling behind the red wheel, with my fingertips playing over the control console. I drove slowly to enjoy the sensation of a new car under me. From time to time I looked at Felicia Marr and smiled.

We were in no hurry to get to Hialiah since we were interested only in the fifth race. I tooled the Starfire along the MacArthur Causeway and onto the Dixie Highway. The top was down, the sun was warm on our flesh, and the car was an automotive masterpiece.

"Let me treat you to lunch," I suggested.

She was leaning with her head back, eyes closed, not caring how her hair was blowing about, just enjoying the warmth and the salt air and the sensation of laziness. Her guard was down. She smiled and agreed to let me do something for her as a change.

"I like the car," I said after a while. "I want to thank you. You've been more than generous."

"I enjoy doing things for you, David," she murmured sleepily. "It gives me a warm feeling."

"Don't you think I enjoy doing things for you?"

"It isn't the same."

I waited a few minutes, then asked, "Does it make you feel insecure, my wanting to do things for you?"

"I don't want to talk about it."

56

"But why not? I mean—"

"Please, David."

Her eyes were still closed so she did not see my shoulders shrug. I put my hand over hers and squeezed. Instantly her fingers wrapped about mine, holding tight. She had the little-girl look back on her face.

"Don't ask questions, David," she whispered. "Just be nice."

"I will."

"Do what I say—what I want you to do."

"Every time."

She held my hand all the way to the race track.

After I parked the car she handed me one thousand, one hundred dollars to put on Futility—in fifty-dollar bills. I saw her to her seat just as the first race was finishing. For kicks, we tried to select winners in the second, third, and fourth. One horse she chose came in second. The rest of our picks were also-rans.

"You sure you want Futility to win?" I asked.

"Oh, yes. Yes, to win."

"We could hedge and bet it to show. With our luck at picking winners it'd be safer."

She looked at me, her eyes purple and hard. They softened after a moment and she patted my hand. "If Futility loses I'll make good what you'd have won."

I jerked my hand away and stood up.

"David, kiss me," she said softly, staring out across the big track. There was a faint smile on her vivid red mouth. I felt no more like kissing her than I felt like playing Russian roulette with a fully loaded revolver.

I bent and kissed her.

On my way to the windows I told myself to bet my hundred as I wanted. Fast Baby was going today in the fifth and was the heavy favorite. I would do no better than break even but at least I'd be in the hundred bucks.

"Hell, it isn't my money," I growled.

I bet the way Felicia wanted me to bet.

Futility won going away. I was on my feet with the rest of the crowd, yelling my throat hoarse, watching the little bay mare come striding to the finish line, two lengths ahead of Fast Baby. Whatever it is in the human make-up that turns people into gamblers was strong in me at that moment. I think I would have taken my winnings—three hundred and fifty smackers—and lost it all on the sixth, seventh and eighth races.

Felicia was too smart for that. She gathered her purse and gloves and stood up as the winning time was posted.

"Cash the tickets, then we'll go," she said.

I opened my mouth to suggest that we stay for at least one more race, that we bet two bucks each, just for the hell of it. She was halfway up the aisle and moving steadily. I went after her, the way I was being trained to do.

She wanted to catch a nap before dinner.

Me, I took a swim in the pool and looked at the girls in their swimsuits and bikinis. The young ones, that is. I caught a few inviting glances but I only smiled and let it go at that. I decided I'd better get back to my room before one of them came over and asked for a match or a cigarette. Felicia Marr was too good a thing to toss over for the sake of a young female body.

No girl was worth it, I told myself.

While I was passing through the arcade, I heard someone call my name. It was Felicia, in the doorway of a plush shop that catered to women guests. You could buy a girdle or an evening gown at any time up to—and maybe even after, for all I knew—midnight. Felicia had decided she needed new clothes.

"There's to be dancing tonight," she told me. "I want to look my best." I wondered if she'd seen me ogling the younger beauties on the rim of the huge pool.

She made me join her on a plush lavender lounge while she made her selections. Not once did she ask my opinion. I was allowed to look at the models who paraded before us in Ceil Chapman and Mainbocher creations, that was all. Not that I minded this sort of thing, you understand, but once in a while you like to be consulted.

We ate Lobster Thermidor in the main dining room and then moved on to the La Ronde, one of two night clubs the Fontainebleau affords. Felicia was in a gay mood, insisting on doing the Twist, the Slop, the Cha-Cha. I give her credit, she was energetic enough for them all. Maybe it was the nap she'd taken after coming back from Hialeah.

After three hours of La Ronde we went to the Boom-Boom Room, a dimly lighted dance floor surrounded by small tables and eager waiters. We drank stingers here instead of the sidecars we'd ordered in La Ronde. The orchestra played soft music, romantic rhythms that had us plastered tight to one another, her cheek on my chest. I could feel her garter clasps against my legs as we moved, and the softness of her loins teasing me.

Her evening gown was black, cut down almost to her buttocks in the back. She wore a pearl necklace and a matching bracelet. They were real pearls and worth at least fifteen thousand dollars. Under all this finery there was only Felicia Marr and a garter belt with gun-metal stockings. She did things to me with her legs and her soft belly, carefully and with calculation. There is a word for a woman like her, rarely used in polite society.

I let her work me over, but I told myself that money or no money, this night I would have either her or one of those young chicks I'd seen around the big pool. If she shut herself up alone in her bedroom, I was going on the town. Either way, I could not lose. So I played her game with her, holding her tight to me, letting her know my need, giving my fingertips permission to roam all over her soft back where the evening gown exposed it.

When we finally drew away from each other she was fighting to control her harsh breathing. "You bastard," she whispered as we walked toward our table. I bowed as I held her chair for her. She meant the word as a compliment. I had succeeded, at last, in getting through to her.

She ordered more stingers.

She wanted to dance again when the orchestra came back, and so did I. I held her tight, so tight I could feel her breasts grow hard against my ribs. Where the room was darkest I slid the tips of my fingers down into her backless evening gown until they were brushing the first swell of her soft buttocks. She was making a scratching sound in her throat by this time and her hips were moving back and forth.

The wheel swings around in any game and now it is my chance to call the turn, you sweet little bitch! I order you, not with my voice but with body, my fingertips and my young male strength. Close your door on me tonight— if you can.

The trouble with all this was that I was driving myself wild, too. My blood bubbled. It was hard to breathe normally. I felt like getting both hands on the shoulder straps of her three-hundred-dollar gown and ripping it the hell off her, right there on the dance floor. Naturally I didn't, but I wanted to.

The next time we went back to the table, I told myself,

if she ordered another round of stingers I'd clobber her. She picked up her purse and gloves and turned on a heel. I went after her, dropping a twenty-dollar bill to cover our drinks and the waiter.

She headed for the elevator.

I went in after her and the door closed with a little sigh of compressed air. She turned to me and lifted her arms. Her eyes were shut and her lips were open just a little. She was vulnerable then.

I could have ignored her and still been safe.

Instead, I put my hands on her and drew her against me and kissed her the way she wanted to be kissed, with my tongue like a flame in her mouth and my body assuring her she was still young, still desirable, still able to drive a young man stark, raving mad with passion.

We clung together, shivering.

SIX

I HELD the bedroom door open for her, taking the purse from her hands, opening it and letting the key fall into its silken interior. She walked with swaying hips into the ornate bedroom and stood waiting for me.

I went up behind her, pressing my mouth to her smooth shoulder. She quivered, pushed back into me and let her head nuzzle mine while I ran my mouth all over her soft throat. My tongue trembled to tell her how much I needed her, that if she put me off tonight I might come close to killing her. I kept quiet. I knew enough about Felicia Marr to understand that in this most intimate of all games between a man and a woman she must show the way.

My hands slid across her hips to her front, stroking her gently. I felt her tremble fitfully. Then I lifted my palms to her breasts. They were as hard as marble through her evening gown.

"Undress me," she breathed.

The black gown slipped easily down her arms to her middle. I kissed her soft back as it fell. She stood like a statue, accepting my homage to her beauty. I could not see her face so I did not know whether she was smiling or frowning but her body was silently screaming its delight with what I was doing. With my lips pressed into the small of her back above the lace and elastic band of her black garter belt, I shoved the dress to her feet.

The sight of her dressed in that black lace thing, those gun-metal nylons, and the high-heeled evening slippers was maddening. She was like a young girl, slim and roundly curved, her smooth skin a creamy gold from the sun except where her trunks had covered her. She was quivering as I bent to kiss her, crying out softly as my mouth roved over her soft flesh.

"Yes," she breathed. "Kiss me, kiss me there!"

I held her thigh as I let my lips adore her beauty. Then I turned her, holding her still while I went on pleasing her. Her lips were open, giving little cries, even as her eyes closed convulsively.

When I let her go at last, she staggered and stared down at me. Hellfires burned deep in her eyes, blazing hot and strangely evil. She bent and let her large breasts slide back and forth across my flushed face.

"Now you, my precious. Take your clothes off."

I was in a trance, held in thrall by the loveliness of her body. Anything this woman wanted of me, I would do. In my crazed state, I was no longer David Mason Horne but manhood incarnate, needing satisfaction of the lusts that make human beings no better, at times, than animals.

She saw my need, my wildness. She laughed triumphantly.

When I stood naked she pointed to her purse where I had tossed it on a chair. "Get me a cigarette, David. Light it for me."

I did what she asked, moving like a sleepwalker. I could no more have resisted her than I could have broken down the walls with my fists. I held a lighter to the cigarette between her lips and bent to touch her shoulder with my mouth.

Felicia was sitting on the edge of the bed. She extended a handsome leg, turning her slippered foot this way and that, relishing my helplessness.

"Take my shoes off, David."

Kneeling before her, I removed them, one after the other. I kissed her stockinged feet, her knees. There was a wildness in her body, and deep in the purple eyes that flared down at me which matched my own. I thought hazily that I could make her as eager, as hypnotically helpless, as I was myself, but I lacked the will power. She was my will power, my backbone, my very moral fiber.

Felicia lay back and stared at the ceiling.

I kissed her as might a slave his mistress, bowing to her

loveliness, attending her beauty with hands and eyes and lips. She made sounds deep in her throat and, after a while, her head began to move back and forth on the bedspread. Her hips jerked and shuddered.

When I stood up to take her she twisted aside and crouched on her hands and knees, glaring at me, shaking her head so her loosened black hair flew back and forth. She made a picture out of Baudelaire, white-and-black naughtiness crouched to spring, to devour.

"No, not me," she breathed. "You, David. You—here!"

She touched the bedspread, patting it where she wanted me.

"Come, dear David. Lie down here on your back. Flat on your back as if you were a beaten fighter. Unable to resist. Helpless to my pleasure."

There was a madness in her voice and in her eyes that should have chilled me, but I was beyond anything but the necessary gratification of my senses. Still in that trance-like state, I lay down so that I stared upward at the ceiling. I felt her hand on me, stroking and caressing.

"This way, David. This way," she breathed.

Her face came between my eyes and the ceiling. Her red wet mouth was open, descending to my lips. She kissed me, forcing her tongue between my teeth. Her hand touched me gently.

"I must be the one to make the moves, you understand," she whispered against my lips. "It isn't any good for me otherwise. And you wouldn't want that, would you, darling?"

"No. No."

She was crawling over my body, caressing it with her own, never taking her eyes from mine. "I am no helpless woman to be enjoyed by a conquering male. Do you realize that? I am the conqueror, the one who takes, when and where I will. It is my pleasure which comes first, ahead of yours."

I could not move a muscle. I lay as if under a spell, pasture for her passions. She went on talking, compelling me to understand that she must dominate, that for Felicia Marr the only enjoyment was that mixed with conquest. She must be the seducer, the taker.

"Sociologists are worrying about women emasculating men, darling—but we aren't, are we? What difference does it make who takes who—to you? Just so long as your pleasure is as great as my own. And it is, isn't it?"

"God, yes," I breathed.

She went on talking even while she surrounded me and lifted me with her into some Nirvana of delight, straddling my loins, smiling down at me, writhing slowly in the sensual delirium in which I was caught up with her.

Psychotic dominance, the casebooks called it—the need of a woman to assert her superiority by masculine tactics, by the submission of her lovers. To avoid yielding to the male, to avoid assuming her normal feminine role, she would fight like a wounded tigress. I only thought of this with a lost corner of my mind—sensing it vaguely like a half-remembered dream—because the rest of me was too lost in a swirl of exquisite sensation.

It did not matter to me what she was or how she got her kicks, right then. Let her dominate, if she needed that psychic satisfaction. It made no never-mind to me. All I cared for was this wild pulsation which gripped me, held me in thrall.

Felicia Marr was an eternity of delight.

And I was sharing in her pleasure.

I spent the night in her bed.

Neither of us was sleepy. I think the need between us had been building since we first saw one another in the airport waiting room and now was the time to satisfy it. I could not get enough of touching her, stroking and kissing her body, making her understand that whatever she wanted from me, she need only ask.

No, not ask. Command.

She told me what to do and how to do it. It was like taking a course in making love with a real gone teacher. She panted and sobbed and even screamed, but she went on ordering me to attend her. I did not realize what she was doing to me, to that part of me that had always been free. It may not have made any difference at that moment. I was consumed with my need for her. She was the flame, I the moth.

And she burned herself deep inside me, where the scars do not show. I was the living dream companion, the bodiless lover in an erotic nightmare, who asked nothing but only gave freely and without obligation of himself and his love.

When we fell asleep, the room was bright with dawn.

From that night on, there was never anything hidden between us. We might have been husband and wife except that neither of us had taken marital vows. Nor did we pretend to one another. It was a silent but admitted fact between us Felicia Marr was the superior. She gave the orders, she paid the bills, she initiated the love-making.

I was having it too good to fight it.

A psychologist might say that mine was the recessive personality, hers the dominant, and in that I would agree. When my adoptive father died and left me penniless through a legal quirk, it had been a hard blow. I was thrust into the world to make my way, utterly unprepared. Had I been younger, I'm positive it would have been what the books call a traumatic experience. Maybe it still was; all I know and am sure of is the fact that I was relieved not to have to work, not be forced to wonder where my next buck was coming from, or even if it was.

Felicia Marr became my lost parent, in a sense.

My bulwark against the world.

All this was not immediately clear to me, of course. The slow realization came over the months we spent together, and with our many intimacies.

Over the breakfast table she told me she was putting me on a salaried basis, two hundred dollars a week and expenses. My only duty was to keep her amused, to prevent her from spending too much time working.

"And to keep me from marrying again," she added slowly, sipping her coffee. "I've had three husbands. I don't want any more."

"Not even Bram Skoronski?"

She put down the cup. "Rhoda told you about him?"

"Is it a secret?"

She shook her head almost imperceptibly. "No, naturally not. Bram wants to marry me but I don't want him." Her eyelids flickered. "Bram is a bull of a man—big, strong, hairy. Any wife of his would have to bow to his wishes, his dictates. I refuse to bow to any man."

She sighed and touched the tablecloth with a red fingernail. "It won't be hard to keep me single, but do it anyhow." The smile she gave me was bright, eager, as if a part of her had decided that it was time now to forget Bram Skoronski and concentrate on enjoying herself. "What do we do today?"

"Hire a boat and go cruising?"

She considered that, head tilted. "All right, I approve of that. I'll climb into toreadors and a sweater. You go make arrangements."

The sun was hot and bright, the waters of Indian Creek cool and green, as our rented Century Raven headed out the channel into the Atlantic. Felicia let me start the motor and ease the Raven away from the wharf. Then she took the wheel and steered our course, competently and surely.

She was like a little girl, laughing and bubbling with delight. The wind tossed her black hair about, tinted her cheeks red on her golden tan. She grew younger by the minute. The spray flecked her yellow, turtle-neck slipover with drops of salt water that glittered like diamonds in the sunlight.

"I don't know when I've had so much fun," she shouted above the roaring motor. Her hand reached for me, drew me toward her on the seat as if she wanted reassurance from the pressure of my body. I put my arm about her middle and held her as the first swelling waves lifted and dropped us into a trough.

She squealed in ecstasy.

Her hand came behind my neck and drew my face to her mouth as she kissed me with open lips and darting tongue. My hand slid under the yellow sweater, found her unbrassiered breast and caressed it.

"For thinking of this, darling," she whispered.

Then she gave her attention to the Century and my hand went back to its post outside the sweater. A hidden voice whispered to me that I had been rewarded like a clever child, been given a sweet and patted on the head. I ignored it.

For the next week Felicia Marr and I had fun.

We went swimming in the ocean and in the Fontaine-bleau pool. I took her to lonely and secluded sand dunes where she could slip out of her suit and sun-bathe in the nude. At night we went dancing in the many night clubs Miami Beach affords. She was stunning in the cocktail gowns she purchased, in the backless dresses in which she went strolling. She actually grew younger as the days went on.

Laughter was always on her lips.

When a big wave tumbled her, her mirth rang out. If she knew that her body was stirring mine as we danced, she chuckled throatily. Even when we were alone in her room, she managed to laugh, that deep sound of desire I had come to know and understand.

65

The fun ended on a Thursday morning.

When we came downstairs together, a stranger to me rose to his feet from one of the lounge chairs in the huge lobby. He was a bear of a man, with black hair cropped to his head, and shoulders a yard wide. I could see at once that Felicia knew him; she came to a dead stop and gasped.

He was moving forward easily, smiling down at her. I could read the delight he felt at sight of her, the affection and regard he had for her, reflected in his eyes. I thought about how little women can twist big men around their little fingers. He ignored me completely, as though I did not exist.

"I came as soon as I could, Lise," he rumbled.

"Why?" she asked coldly.

Momentarily he looked deflated but he thought too much of himself to remain that way for very long. His big hand came to her arm, to turn her toward the dining room. "Let's eat. I'm starved. Couldn't swallow a thing all the way down."

"You go ahead, Bram. David and I have other plans."

So this was Bram Skoronski. I let my eyes weigh him, knowing that with his muscular bulk I would be no match for him in any slugging bee. Confidence oozed from his every pore. He was a man who got his own way in everything, thanks to a blend of good looks, personal charm, and the driving force that had made him a millionaire at the age of thirty. In his forties now, he had kept his body in perfect condition while adding to his wealth by manipulations in the stock market.

Any other woman would look on him as a perfect catch. Not Felicia Marr. Bram Skoronski was a man she could not dominate. In his bullheadedness, he would neither see nor understand the sort of woman she was. Perhaps he did not care; it would be enough for him that he wanted her and meant to get her, one way or another.

He grinned down at her as anyone else might at an impish child whose behavior patterns are amusing. Felicia Marr was not so much a person in his eyes as a problem in human relations to be solved. Long used to dealing with people, used also to getting his own way, he could not believe she really meant what she said.

"Bring your little friend along. I'll stand treat."

"Oh, Bram. Now honestly!"

For the first time he seemed to grow aware of my existence. He turned from Felicia, slowly, to stare at me. The amusement had faded from his face. His eyes were black and hard and cold. They lifted me, turned me around to study me, then dismissed me. He swung back to Felicia.

"I wrangled a couple of days off for myself, Lise. I couldn't think of a better way to spend them than with you."

She smiled sweetly. "Darling, how touching." He did not sense her sarcasm but preened himself as though she were paying him a compliment. I had the feeling that Bram Skoronski was a smart, tough man except where Felicia Marr was concerned. She was his one blind spot.

Felicia put her hand in mine and brushed Bram with a shoulder as she went past him. I shot one glance at his startled face. He knew what was happening, then; but he could not accept it. He came after us, matched his long strides with ours.

"Maybe you didn't understand, Lise. I said I came all the way down here to spend a few days with you. The Long Hills spring tourney is coming up and I figured we'd get in a couple of rounds of golf."

Felicia Marr halted. She turned her face up toward him. "Maybe you didn't understand, Bram Skoronski," she said softly. "I haven't the slightest desire to spend any more time with you here in Miami Beach than it takes to tell you I don't want to see you. Go get lost. Or go home. I'm on a holiday. I have to see you back in Westport, since you're in our set. I don't have to see you while on a vacation."

This was straight from the shoulder stuff that he could understand. His face flushed the color of a brick under its tan. He stiffened and his wide mouth set in a firm, grim line. There was agony in his eyes, though, which Felicia ignored.

"Do you get the message, Bram?"

He tried to laugh, but it was a weak effort. His glance touched me and a cold chill ran down my spine. Bram Skoronski blamed me for this thing that was eating in his woman, in his Felicia Marr; I had done something to change her over into a petulant female. If we'd been alone, I think he would have ruined my face with his fists—or killed me.

I tried to imagine what it would be like to fight this human grizzly bear. I shivered and stopped thinking about it.

"Bram?" she pressed. "Do you understand?"

"Sure. You want to be alone with lover boy. He's pretty enough, I guess. And fun. How much are you paying him?"

I opened my mouth to protest but I closed it when I realized I would be playing into his hands. He itched for an excuse to slap me around. Let me make the first move, just one single threatening gesture, and he would be on me with both hamlike fists, hammering hard. He was even holding his breath with anticipation.

"Apologize, Bram," Felicia said sharply.

I held my breath as I saw the ugliness creep into his features. A growl started in his throat but he must have thought better of whatever it was he might have said just then. He turned his head and looked at Felicia. His smile was sickly.

"Right, Lise. I'm sorry," he said slowly.

He was apologizing to her, not to me, but Felicia seemed to realize she would be unable to push him any farther. She merely caught my arm and walked me out of the lobby into the sunlight.

"Let's have breakfast someplace else this morning," she said. "I just couldn't eat knowing he was sitting at a nearby table staring at us. I'd have an unpleasant taste in my mouth."

We stopped for fruit juice and coffee, then back to the Fontainbleau. A discreet inquiry gave us to understand that Bram Skoronski had checked out an hour after he'd signed the register. There was a plane for New York leaving at noon; the desk clerk had made arrangements for him to be on it. His luggage would follow him north.

"Thank God," breathed Felicia. "I thought my vacation was ruined." In an excess of high spirits, she danced across the lobby. "Take me somewhere lonely, David— somewhere we can be alone."

There was a memo waiting for her at the desk when we got back to the Fontainbleau. New York had called. It was urgent. Would she like the operator to call back? New York had left a number.

"The office," she sighed. "Wouldn't you know?"

She made the call from the vanity bench in the dressing room after I had plugged in the phone. Her hand made signs at me as I was running the water for her bath. I got a cigarette, put it between her lips and lighted it for her.

"Hello? Hello? Murchison? What's wrong?"

She listened awhile, frowning, puffing on the cigarette. Tiny beads of perspiration flecked her forehead. She made more signs, lifted her arms. The yellow slipover was too hot. I drew it off her head and she sat, naked to the waist, listening to the sounds coming through the receiver.

When she spoke, it was with an entirely different voice than she had let me hear so far—decisive, authoritative, almost angry. I did not follow her too well. It was something about a competitor underselling some item which one of her factories produced. She told Murchison exactly what she wanted done.

" . . . new advertising campaign. Feature the quality of our product, its longevity. I don't care whether it wears better or not. Say it does. What? Oh, hell. I can't be bothered with—no, no. Go ahead, I'll listen."

Her eyes rolled when she saw me looking at her, and her lips made silent words. He—wants—me—to—come—home. She gave a little shrug and her breasts jumped slightly. Squirming around on the vanity bench, she rubbed out the cigarette in a glass ash tray.

"All right, Murch. You win," she said resignedly. "I'll come back. Yes, yes. Tomorrow, by plane. Oh—tell Dori, will you? She'll need to know. So I can handle it myself, yes. I understand. And thanks for calling."

She hung up and slapped the vanity top with a palm. "Christ damn it. And I was having such a good time, too!" She glanced sideways at me. "Can you keep me entertained up north, honey?"

I knelt and put my hands on her big, heavy breasts, stroking them slowly until they grew hard in my palms. I told her I could entertain her anywhere. So she had to go back to New York. It wasn't the end of our world together, only one phase of it.

Her eyes were closed and she was smiling when I stopped talking. Gently she disengaged my hands, pushing them away. "Thanks, lover. You have made me feel better. Mmm, don't know what I'd do without you. You're a doll. Is my bath ready?"

She got to her feet and began to slide her toreadors down. I said slowly, "The only place to go if you want a real vacation is Europe. Keep on the go. Never stay long in the same place."

I held her arm while she balanced on one foot and tested the warmth of the bath waters with the other. "Europe. Now there's an idea." She sank into the tub,

69

reached for a cake of soap. "I think I'd like a trip to Europe right about now. I haven't been in five, six years. Too busy."

She was running the soap over her breasts, making frothy bubbles, smiling as if to secret thoughts. "Europe can be fun if one knows where to go." She touched me with her eyes. "Do you know where to go, David?"

I nodded, remembering Capri and its blue grotto, the Positano Beach near Naples where the girls wore the smallest bikinis this side of the French Riviera. I thought about the gondolas of Venice and a big yellow moon shining down on its gurgling canal waters, the sidewalk cafés in Rome. It would be fun going back to all those places with Felicia.

"Tell me," she said, "tell me all about them."

While she bathed I told her about the *vieux port* section of Marseilles, which was slowly coming back to its old popularity as a red-light district where anything went for enough money. The Germans had dynamited it because the French Resistance people hid out there, but time had healed those pockmarked wounds. The Cannebiere was still noted for its little bistros, where *bouillabaisse* was almost a religion.

If she wanted something a little out of the ordinary we might sample Tuborg beer in Copenhagen or those open sandwiches called *smorrebrod,* of which the Danes were so justly proud. There were so many places to have fun in Europe: London boasted its private clubs like The Irving and Winston's, or niteries like the Windmill; Paris its own haunts such as the Crazy Horse Saloon, the Club Sexy, the Grisby Club. Unfortunately, the authorities had closed the Sphinx but the word was out that there were other night spots just as exciting.

Felicia listened with her mouth a little open, her eyes wide, forgetting to use the soap. I told her about the Reeperbahn in Hamburg, a sin street de luxe, where anything goes, from nude shows to audience participation orgies—a square half-mile of undiluted vice. I touched lightly on the Moulin Rouge in Vienna and Le Boule Blanche in Paris. There were others I didn't mention, little out of the way cellars where you could become part of the floor show if you had such inclinations.

"How long has this been going on?" she asked after a while. "You're so young. You couldn't have gotten them all in, by yourself."

"I had friends," I grinned. "The friends got me in and I paid the tab. I had a big allowance in those days."

"Do you still have your admission cards?"

I made a little bow.

We did not go down to the main dining room that night. Instead, we used room service, ordering steak à deux, tossed salad and coffee, which we ate over a service table, Felicia in her black gauze nightgown, I in my silk pajamas.

"I have to be more or less circumspect back in New York, darling," she informed me. "This is our last night together for a little while. My staff keeps close tabs on me."

"Your staff?"

"Doctor Vance. Dori Pierce, my secretary. Even my cook. I am allowed to do only so many things per week. One show, one local movie perhaps. I can eat out three times at night. Four nights a week I must be in bed by ten. Under sedation, if I'm not sleepy."

"Now I know why you hired me," I laughed. "You need somebody to think up ways and means of eluding your jailers."

"If only you could," she sighed ecstatically, and clasped her fingers together. "My darlings mean well but they're utter tyrants. They have my health in mind, but sometimes I think there's such a thing as being too healthy."

I studied her as she lay back in the chaise longue in that black mist robe that made her nakedness the more tantalizing because it was partially hidden. White flesh under black gauze always was exciting to me. I watched as she leaned forward, studying the sway of her heavy breasts pressing into the lace bodice, brown nipples rigid, the round swells pallid and waiting. Her legs stirred lazily as she shifted position. Her belly trembled gently. Now I could see the curve of a hip, part of a pale buttock.

She smiled, seeing where my eyes went.

"I feel pretty healthy right now, David. Why don't you come over here and find out just how healthy?"

I sat beside her on the chaise, caressed her gently with my hand. She leaned her head into the crook of my arm and began to talk.

"You have the nicest hands, David. I enjoy their touch on me so much. Ooooh, yes—especially there. Mmmmm. So nice. I need no sedatives when you're around. Darling, darling, darling . . ."

She twisted, writhing as my hand fondled her, beginning

71

to moan deep in her throat. I slid the nightgown down to her waist, bent to kiss her swollen breasts, laving the nipples with my tongue. Her hands grew restless, moved to me, caressing my body gently, hungrily.

We were in no hurry. We let our bodily pleasure build slowly, for we had the whole night before us. For half an hour we continued our caresses until we were flushed and feverish with desire. Then Felicia pushed me away, telling me to phone room service for drinks.

"Let's calm down for a while, sweetikins," she breathed.

Her big breasts were naked outside the nightgown, which was bunched about her pale hips. She made no move to hide herself from my eyes. She was calling the play and it had to go her way or not at all. I was on fire but I told myself to be patient, that everything comes to him who waits. She looked a little disappointed when I reached for the phone and ordered a pitcher of martinis. Maybe she wanted me to attack her so she could prove her mastery.

I used the fifteen minutes until the waiter knocked on our door to rouse her unmercifully. She was panting thickly, crying out softly at what I was doing to her. She was damn well ready to explode, hips moving and legs opening and closing.

It was then that the waiter knuckled the door.

I put on my dressing robe and went to the door with a twenty-dollar bill, trading it for the pitcher and frosted glasses on a tray. As the door closed behind the waiter, I knew that Felicia had quieted down just enough to keep me waiting some more.

She drank most of the martinis, letting me have only two, telling me that too much liquor was no good for a boy like me at a time like this. She smiled when she said it but I could see the power shining in her eyes. She had me on a hot spot and she meant to keep me dangling to prove she was my superior.

I let her prove it to me for another hour of interrupted caresses. Once she said her hair was mussed and she insisted on setting it back in place. Another time she asked me to get her a cigarette. I was pretty wild by this time.

I guess she understood how it was with me, all right. She pointed toward the bed, finally, and told me to go lie down. On my back, the way I had to be with her. She came toward me, lifting off her nightgown, baring her body for my eyes.

She crawled on top of me and took me.

SEVEN

I DROVE the Starfire north to New York by way of U.S. 1 and the Jersey Turnpike. I was in no hurry. I figured that by this time the big DC-6B plane would have touched down at LaGuardia and Felicia Marr would be sitting behind her Saarinen desk in the United Oils Building. I let the powerful Olds cruise along at sixty and basked in the springtime sun.

Naturally, I wondered if I was doing the right thing. It was all well and good to work for Felicia Marr at two hundred a week and expenses. For that money I was giving up my independence, surrendering my psychic self as well as my body, every time she took me to bed.

I would be an idiot to turn down her offer, I told myself. Two hundred a week and expenses wasn't to be laughed at by a young man who had no training to do anything else. There was no permanence to the job, however. Let Felicia tire of me and I was out on my ear.

Harsh laughter grated in my throat.

I would be no worse off then than now, except that I'd be a little older. The smart thing for me to do would be get a job with some sort of future. Hell, I could even go to law school for the next three years with the money Felicia Marr had given me; train myself to enter the legal department of some big corporation. Then, at least, I could look around for a wife, marry and settle down, become respectable.

It sounded good in my head. Actually, it was nonsense.

I was no scholar. Not for me the hours of study, the single-mindedness of purpose needed for a law degree. And for what? To become one more suburban commuter? A cog in the corporate image? Not when there was an easier way to do it.

I ate at one of the Howard Johnson restaurants that dot the Turnpike, enjoying my freedom, the liberty of driving north without a worry on a Wednesday afternoon. How many men, slaving their heads off in mundane jobs, would trade places with me? More than you might suspect, I'd bet.

I had it made. Why was I griping?

Maybe it was my male pride, so long forgotten, making itself heard. Last night Felicia Marr had made me feel like a male whore, somebody hired to pleasure her body when

73

she felt like it, to dance attendance on her, to jump through psychological hoops when she snapped her fingers.

"Hell," I grumbled to myself. "Stop bitching."

The waitress came up with my sandwich and coffee, giving me a funny look. I grinned at her, saying, "I got troubles, honey."

She smiled, nodding. "You're one of us, mister."

Everybody had troubles, she as good as said. The thing was, troubles comes in degrees. When I thought of it like that, mine didn't seem so bad. At least I could eat in the best places, wear the finest clothes, sleep between the freshest sheets, and bed down with a most attractive woman. Everybody should have troubles like that, I thought. I laughed and began to eat.

The Starfire was on the George Washington Bridge by three o'clock in the afternoon, moving steadily north along the Henry Hudson Parkway. I was heading for the Marr place in Westport, Connecticut. Felicia hadn't seemed enthusiastic about my picking her up at her office, so I held straight to my course for the Cross County Parkway and the Merritt. The day was warm and sunny. The Starfire top was down, and my body was alive to the budding trees and green grass all around me.

This same mood of awareness, of eagerness and anticipation, was still in me as I swung off the parkway at the Westport exit, past the Red Barn and along Wilton Road. Tonight I would be sleeping in what would be my future home instead of a Virginia motel.

The house came at you through a private road lined with big oaks. A huge old-fashioned building of red brick and white woodwork with tall windows, it had been modernized by the addition of a glass wall and a matching wing. As I braked the Olds in the graveled area before the old stable converted into a garage, I saw that there was more of the house toward the rear. Even without the new addition, the place was imposing; with it, it seemed the size of a small hotel.

Off to one side, past a small park area, there was an old barn, the one Felicia had made over into a studio apartment. To add to the décor, a fieldstone well stood just beyond it. A flagstone path connected the drive-in area with the studio.

I swung my bag from the trunk, walked to the back door. An older woman came and stared at me. She was the family cook, Elvira; I recognized her from what Felicia had told me about her. She was not small and plump and motherly the way I always envisioned family cooks but lean and small, on the wiry side.

Suddenly she smiled and her face changed to an almost-prettiness. "You're David. Lise phoned about you, said you'd be in sometime today. Come in, come in. Put down your bag. Any place will do. You're hungry, aren't you?"

She appeared to have that compulsion common to many women who regard their cooking ability as a status symbol. What she lacked in looks—or maybe in a bed, for all I knew—she got back when she worked with pots and pans. I had the feeling that her food just might be everything she thought it.

"I could do with a sandwich but dinner's not far off and—"

"Miss Lise never eats before eight. Tonight she won't be home until nine or ten. She's dining in the city."

I began taking off my coat. "Just show me where to wash up and I'm your boy," I told her.

We took to one another right away. While I washed and she puttered around with ham and eggs and Danish pastry, she told me what I wanted to know about the staff and about life in Felicia Marr's Westport.

"There's just Benjie and me here," she said, frothing scrambled eggs. "Benjie's a sort of butler and handyman rolled up in one. He does the outside work, I do the inside, 'cept when there's house guests and he has to put on a uniform and buttle."

Benjie Warren was in his fifties, the possessor of a high school diploma—he had been a star athlete for a local high school back in the Twenties, but had never gone on to college. "Family needed him. His pa died, his ma was never a well woman. Benjie worked around town, ran a haberdashery for a while, became a bartender when saloons came back into style, and drove a delivery truck. He's handy with tools. He fixed Lise's car one day when it had engine trouble, stopping his truck to do it. She hired him on the spot."

"What about you?" I smiled.

She gave me a brief smile. "Me, I came with the house. Family owned it ages ago. I had to sell to make ends meet. Lise and me, we got friendly on her visits from the city when she was trying to make up her mind to buy. She tasted my cooking and offered me a job as cook." She gave a brief laugh and her hands paused while she stared out over the green fields westward of the house. "I like it fine. It's almost like I never sold. I kept my old room. I cook her meals and mine and for an occasional guest.

"When she isn't here, which is most of the time, I pretend it's still mine. She's left the house to me in her will, did you know that? Isn't that wonderful of her? I get to keep the purchase money and it's as if nothing ever happened. Of course, she did add to it, the new wing and all, but that makes the property more valuable, wouldn't you say?"

I said so enthusiastically as she set the platter of ham and scrambled eggs in front of me. They had been frothed with wine and had a delicate flavor which I'd never before sampled. I praised her cooking with even more gusto and made myself a friend.

"Doesn't life get a little lonely for you here? Alone most of the time?"

She smiled faintly, leaning against the big modern sink, watching me eat. "I got Doc Vance. He's an old friend. We used to go 'round together back in high school and college days. Doc married a girl from Greenwich—her family had money—and for a time we lost track of one another. When Felicia moved here we had to call in a doctor, and who showed up but Thurlow. It was like old times."

Her face seemed puzzled, but only for an instant, so that I told myself I imagined that odd look. She said slowly, "His wife died three, four years ago. He's a widower." It was as if Elvira wondered why he never asked her to marry him, now that the way was clear. "We go to movies, to an occasional New York show, and driving on his day off."

I looked at Elvira Bennett in a new light, as a woman who might have a lover in Doctor Vance. She was on the lean side but not scrawny, by any means. There was meat on her bones, her legs were handsome and her hips gently curved. The shapeless housedress she wore did nothing for her figure, but from time to time as she moved I saw its bodice mound out under the pressure of a breast. At least she wasn't flat up there where it counted.

"There's Dori, too, isn't there? Felicia's secretary?"

"Dori Pierce. I don't know too much about her. She's a quiet thing, almost mousy—Keeps watching Lise out of the corners of her eyes when Lise isn't looking her way—as if . . . if she were afraid of her in some way."

I thought about what Rhoda Travis had told me of Felicia Marr. *She destroys everything and everyone she touches.* Maybe she was in the process of destroying Dori Pierce. I wondered vaguely if it would ever come my turn to be destroyed.

Elvira went on talking. "She's been to college—Sarah Lawrence, I think. She's a good secretary. I've heard men guests offer her a job with them at more pay. She always turns them down. Of course, she lets Felicia hear about it so she gets a pay hike, but I suppose she's worth it."

She glanced at me slyly. "Don't you want to hear about Bram Skoronski?" There was an air about her of a cat licking its chops.

"I've already met him, thanks," I replied.

She moved from the sink, drew out a chair, and sat across the breakfast nook table from me. "Tell me about it. Did he follow her to Miami Beach?"

I told her about it.

When I was done, she shook her head. "He'll make trouble yet for her. And maybe for you, too. You'll see. He's a mean man, that Bram."

I shivered, suddenly cold.

Felicia Marr came into the house with a swirl of cold night air, calling out, tossing her John Frederics hat one way, her gloves another. I had been reading in the old living room. I got up and went to meet him. She moved right into my arms, kissing me, hugging me to her, oblivious of the fact that a woman was with her, watching us with wide, dark eyes.

"This is Dori, David," Felicia said as she pushed me away. "Be friends, you two. I lean on each of you. Oooh, my head."

She had a hand to her temple, massaging the skin with her fingertips, making a wry face. "I've had this headache all day. Tensions, tensions. Dori, be a dear and get my pills—no, wait. Doctor Vance. Get him over here right away."

Obediently, Dori moved to the hall phone and dialed a number. I watched her, wondering a little. She was an attractive girl, but she made herself up to look like a sexless robot. Her black hair was pulled straight back from her forehead and worked into a bun at the base of her neck. Thick black hornrims gave her a scholarly look. She wore no lipstick. Her plain gray-flannel suit fitted a good figure

but her blouse was rumpled and spotted with fallen cigarette ashes.

It struck me oddly that she was in disguise.

"Hello? Doctor Vance? Oh."

She turned to Felicia where she was sitting in a wing
chair, her head back against its rest, eyes closed. "The doctor's at the hospital. Something about an emergency
appendectomy."

"Get the hospital. Tell him to come over here."

Dori turned back to the phone, began dialing the
hospital.

I walked over in front of Felicia, saying, "I have some
bromo in my bag. I never travel without it. Let me get
you some."

"I want Doctor Vance," she said dully.

We could hear Dori talking in the hall, swiftly, unemo-
tionally. "She wants you, Doctor. No, only you. No, she
won't take the pills. She wants you here. Right away. Yes,
I'll tell her." There was a little pause, then Dori said more
loudly, "Felicia, the doctor is just about to operate on a
patient with a burst appendix. If he doesn't operate now,
the child may die."

"Get him over here, damn you. Get him over here!"

Felicia came upright in the chair, hammering its arm
with a clenched fist. Her face was flushed, her eyes brilliant. Anger contorted her usually placid features.

"Oh, Christ damn it! I'll talk to him myself," she
screamed. Her hand pushed me back as she bounced from
the chair and moved into the hall. She wrenched the phone
from Dori—who watched her quietly, moving back a step
to be out of her way—then snapped at the mouthpiece.

"Doc? Felicia. Goddamn it, man, when I tell you I need
you, you hump yourself to get over here. Fast. You understand that, goddamn you? None of your icky excuses. What
do I care about some sick kid? I need you now."

She slammed the phone back in its cradle, leaning her
head against the wall, breathing scratchily. "Bastard knows
I like him around when my head gets like this. Why's he
always running off to that bitchy hospital? Probably some
roundheel nurse waiting for him with her pants down."

She sneered at Dori, then moved past her toward the
staircase. Me, she ignored. Over her shoulder she called
back, "When he gets here, send him up. I'll be waiting."

I stared after her, then turned to the girl.

Dori Pierce was calmly hanging up her spring coat in

the hall closet. Her face was smooth and unruffled, as though her employer had not thrown a violent temper tantrum. When she felt my eyes on her she stared back owlishly through her black-rim glasses. There was absolutely no expression on her face.

Without acknowledging my presence, she swept past me and up the stairs. I went back to my book in the living room but I found myself staring blankly at the printed pages. Felicia Marr needed to dominate, there was no doubt about that. This was as the very air to her lungs. Her word must bring men and women running to attend, either her sexual needs or some other bodily irritation. Maybe her psychic self was fed by the prompt obedience of those around her. A man like Bram Skoronski would not kowtow to her; he was too strong a character.

I smiled grimly. Neither would Doctor Vance, I'd bet.

I was wrong. In half an hour the front doorbell chimed. Dori Pierce ran to open the door.

"Doctor? She's that way again," I heard her say breathlessly.

"The child I left may die. Does she understand that?"

They came into the living room. Doctor Thurlow Vance was a dark, heavy-set man with black hair cut in a crew, heavily tanned and thick through the shoulders. His eyes were black, his face deeply furrowed. His bushy eyebrows rose at sight of me. When Dori introduced us, he grunted and turned toward the stairs.

I waited a little while, then went up myself. The door to her bedroom—it was in the new wing and occupied all one floor— was open. The rest of the house was silent and their voices carried easily.

"The child won't die, so stop worrying about it."

"Luckily for her one of the resident physicians could take over."

"Just what I said," Felicia pronounced triumphantly.

"It's the principle of the thing I object to. You merely have a headache. It could have waited a couple of hours. Those pills I gave you were just as good as what I did."

"Don't disparage yourself, Thurlow."

There was a little silence. Judging by the sounds, Doctor Vance was putting things back inside his black bag. I moved closer. Felicia was sitting up in bed in a night-gown, her hair being put in curlers by Dori Pierce. There was a triumphant smile on her mouth. She watched Vance as a cat watches a bird before it pounces.

When he snapped the bag shut, she said sweetly, "It's nice to know I have two such wonderful friends as you and Dori, Thurlow. I do appreciate it. I want you to know that. It's especially comforting to know that your attendance on me will go on and on—and on."

"Until death do us part," murmured Dori tonelessly.

Felicia let her laughter ring out. "Darling, you're priceless. We're wedded together, in a sense—the three of us. I like that. Yes! All for one—me." Her laughter made a cold chill run down my spine. I wanted very much to see the faces of those other two in the room with her, but I was afraid to come any closer.

I drew a deep breath. I didn't know what was going on but I knew one thing for sure: I wanted not to be seen by any of them, eavesdropping as I was. I moved along the thick carpeting of the hall to the stair and down to the first floor.

I was reading when Doctor Vance left. He came downstairs alone, picked up his coat and stamped out. He was like a wounded rhino, moving straight ahead, daring anything to stand in his path. I maintained a discreet silent.

Dori Pierce came down a little after midnight.

"Felicia wants to know if you've seen your room yet?"

"Not yet but I'd like to. My eyes feel like fried peppers." I grinned, trying to entice her mouth into an answering smile. No dice. I told myself this dame could not be the emotionless dish she seemed.

"I'll show you up," she announced. "You'll want to kiss Felicia good night. We'll stop by on the way."

I kissed Felicia good night while Dori watched. Her eyes staring at me made two cold spots on either side of my spine. If it hadn't been for her, I might have made more of a production of our kiss because Felicia was propped up against some fancy pillows, wearing a flimsy pink nightgown that was no more than a cloud over her big white breasts. I forgot my tiredness looking down into the cleavage she was showing.

She smiled knowingly at me and wrinkled her nose. "See you tomorrow, angel. Get a good night's sleep. You'll be playing golf by ten."

This was news to me. She caught my hand, tugged me down beside her. "We're playing together Sunday in a club tournament. Mixed doubles. Bram Skoronski wanted me to be his partner. He likes to win all the time. Last year he and I won quite handily, but he's been a trifle

80

annoying lately so I turned him down. I entered your name instead. You do play, don't you?"

"Fairly well," I nodded.

In my college years I'd been a runner-up in the N.C.A.A. golf tourney and captain of the team in my senior year. I said nothing of this to Felicia; I thought it might be a pleasant surprise. I was no match physically for the bigger, heavier Bram Skoronski but maybe with a golf club in my hand I could hold my own with him.

"I don't care about winning," she told me. "It doesn't mean that much." She did not need to say so; I understood her clearly enough; all she wanted was to punish Skoronski for his presumption by not playing with him.

Her hand patted my cheek. "I'm tired, dear. Dori will show you to your room. When your trunk arrives I'll have Elvira put your things away. Right now you'll have to live out of your bag. If there's anything you need, see Dori."

I leaned to kiss her again.

Then I was following Dori Pierce down the hall and to a stairway that lowered into the old part of the house, to a floor where three bedrooms flanked a narrow hall. The first door was that of her room, she informed me. The room next to it was empty. Mine was the final one; it overlooked the park to the rear of the house; in the daytime it was sunny and warm, at night there was always a breeze in case I liked to sleep with my windows open.

I thanked her and told her it would be nice sharing the floor with her. She stared through me. So far I hadn't seen her smile once. I shrugged and opened my bedroom door, switched on the light, and closed the door behind me.

At nine o'clock next morning I was on the first tee of the Long Hills Country Club course. I'd never played Long Hills, so I looked forward to the experience. If I was to be at my best the following day—and I wanted desperately to be, if only because of Bram Skoronski—I had to familiarize myself with the layout.

I started slowly, taking a five on the first hole, a four on the second. Then my swing came back to me, my irons behaved, and my putts started dropping just right. I finished with a seventy-nine—seven over par.

It was a little past one. I ate in the Club Room, using Felicia's credit card. She had already phoned the manager to clear me. I was there as a guest, but she'd informed me that she would arrange for my membership if I wanted.

I wanted, all right. With practice I could take this course in the high sixties. Long Hills was not nearly as hard as the Merion or Pinehurst courses. It had nothing to compare with the 11th hole at the North Carolina layout or the rugged 5th at Pine Valley.

After lunch I went out for another eighteen holes. I chopped my score down by eight, to a respectable seventy-one. I would have liked a full week to play the course but I had to learn it in a rush job. I studied the sand traps, the woods to the right of the tenth hole, the fairways and the roughs. The greens were fast this early in the year.

Felicia Marr wanted to chop Bram Skoronski down to size?

So did I.

When I got back to the house, Felicia was working in the light, airy office in the new wing. I put my clubs—a set of matched woods, irons and putter in a cowhide bag, which Felicia had ordered for me as soon as Bram Skoronski reminded her about the Spring Tournament—in my room, then stretched out on the bed. I went over the course again, hole by hole, visualizing it as it had been under my shoes a few hours earlier.

The traveling clock on my night table said seven o'clock.

It must be time to eat, my stomach told me.

I swung off the bed, undressed and showered, then climbed into something more formal than golf slacks and a sweater. When I was done it was close to eight. I went out into the hall and closed the door.

I started down the hall. I stopped.

The door into Dori Pierce's room was open. She was standing there with her head tilted back, the neck of a fifth of DeWars Scotch whiskey held between her lips. I could see the contents level go down as she swallowed steadily. I whistled softly in admiration.

She lowered the bottle and stared over it at me.

Then she said something unprintable.

EIGHT

DINNER WAS a quiet affair. Felicia had been working hard all day, catching up on the desk work she had missed by running off to Miami Beach. She was tired and there were dark patches under her eyes. She made light of them, maybe to prevent me from making any comment. She kept looking at Dori from time to time, the tiny smile in evidence on her mouth.

Dori was half stoned, eating at the table. She kept her eyes on her plate and on her water glass. She looked neither at Felicia nor at me. I saw a nerve quiver in her throat whenever Felicia spoke to her, so I knew she was not as oblivious to her surroundings as she made out.

I kept the conversation going, such as it was. I talked about the country club course and some of the other nines I'd played. Felicia was pleasantly surprised to find me so knowledgeable and sat up straighter, some of the old sparkle coming back into her eyes.

"Do you think we have a chance to win?" she asked finally.

"I intend to win," I said bluntly.

Her purple eyes danced in glee. "Even with the great Bram Skoronski, the club champion, as your opponent?"

"Can you handle his partner, whoever she is?"

"Celia Dawes. If she's real hot she'll go under eighty. I shoot between eighty and ninety. Usually we finish just about even, give or take a few strokes."

I nodded, content. All I asked was a fighting chance.

"In that case," she went on, putting her napkin beside her place setting, "I'm going to bed right now. I'll even take a couple of sleeping pills. I don't want to poop out about the sixteenth hole tomorrow. Dori, darling—don't stay out late."

Dori made no reply. At a signal from Felicia I got to my feet and went with her into the hall, where she turned to me. "She's got half a bun on. Nights like this she goes the rounds of the taverns. I'll give you a list of them. You may have to go after her if she isn't in by one." ·

I said I'd sack in early and set the alarm for that time. If she wasn't in her room I'd go hunting. Felicia patted my arm, smiling up at me.

When I went back to the table, Dori was gone.

I ate Peach Melba and drank coffee alone.

The alarm drew me out of a dreamless sleep to the awareness of moonlight in my room. Blindly I reached out and stabbed at the control rod. I shook my head groggily. One o'clock in the morning? Now why in hell had I made such a mistake? I was off by seven hours.

Oh! Dori Pierce.

I walked barefoot and in my pajamas out of my room

and into hers. The room was empty, the bed neatly made. Under my breath I told Dori Pierce what I thought about her. Nothing to do now but go back, get dressed, take the Starfire and begin making the rounds of the taverns. I hoped that while I dressed I'd hear her little Volvo putter up the drive. No such luck.

I wheeled out the Olds and drew the list of tavern shops from my pocket. *Ready or not, Dori darling, here I come.* I made four stops before I found her perched on a high stool in a bar known as The Red Clock. Her arms were resting on the bartop, her hands cupped about a cock-tail glass. She looked like a strait-laced schoolteacher whose laces were coming undone.

The box jacket to her gray-flannel business suit was thrown back, exposing a white blouse into which two ample breasts in a strong brassiere thrust heavy mounds. Wide hips in a slim, tight skirt all but overflowed the bar stool. The bun in which she had twisted her black hair had come loose so that a lock dangled down beside her horn-rim glasses. Her lips were loose and wet.

I snaked a leg over the stool next to her and ordered bourbon on the rocks. I waited for her to look at me. She went on staring at the liquor in her glass. She could have been dead, sitting there, but she wasn't. She spoke after a while.

"Get to hell out of here," she said tonelessly.

"Why, Dori—how you talk."

"Go on back to her. Give her what she's hired you for. I'll bet you're pretty good at that, aren't you?"

I ignored the crack. I said, "You've been around tonight."

"I intend to keep on going, too."

"Uh-uh, honey. Time to go as soon as you finish."

"You're going to make me?"

For the first time she turned her head and looked at me. Her eyes were miserable, sick, and her features made a caricature of a woman whose soul was dead inside her. Her full red lips trembled and she seemed on the verge of tears.

Suddenly I was embarrassed, as if I'd been caught peep-ing at her during an intimate moment. I took refuge be-hind my bourbon glass and thought fast.

"Look, this isn't my idea," I told her. "Felicia said to come after you, to bring you back."

She put a hand on mine. Her palm was hot, dry, and the manner in which her fingers tightened on me told me

84

she was afraid. "I'm not blaming you, not really. It's her. She owns us all. You, me, Doctor Vance."

I kept my mouth shut. This was news to me, but I nodded. Apparently I looked sympathetic enough to suit her because she went on after drawing a deep breath.

"Six years I've been with her now. Six years of hell. Just hell. For the doc, it's been even more than that—nine or maybe ten, I'm not sure. Six years. God! I've thought about killing her. Nights I lie awake, dreaming up ways, ways that'll get me off the hook and her into her coffin. I've never been able to come up with anything, though."

"You don't read enough murder mysteries."

"Oh, but I do. I read three, four a week. There's nothing in any of them to help me. I keep on reading and hoping."

I tried to make my side of it light. "Let me know when you do. I'll be sure to have a good alibi."

The eyes behind her lenses went over me. "You're still young. Maybe you can get out. What's she got on you?"

"I like money. She pays me good wages." Suspicion was alive in her as she stirred restlessly on the bar stool. Her hand went away from me and closed around her glass.

"I'm not prying. I don't care if you want to clam up about it. I'll learn sooner or later, anyhow. My job as her personal secretary gives me an opportunity to get at all her private papers. All except my own. The bitch. The utter *bitch!* I hate her goddamn guts."

She finished her drink. I did the same, then put a hand on her wrist. "Let's go, honey. This won't get you anything."

"It usually makes me forget. It isn't working tonight. Maybe I need something stronger than a drink."

She smiled crookedly, looking at me. Then she turned on the stool, nudging her silken knee into my groin. She moved it gently, back and forth, still with that loose-lipped smile on her face. She slid off the stool and put her belly against me.

"All right, David. Take me home."

Sure, I should have pushed her away, remembered she was crocked, that she had problems. Instead I put my arm around her middle and gave her a squeeze, just enough so that she would understand I wasn't insensible to her charms. She put out her tongue, licked her lips slowly.

I paid the tab with a ten-spot and guided her across the dimly lit bar and out into the cool night air. Her body was soft under the business suit, and redolent of musky perfume. Her feet had trouble going where she wanted them to, but maybe that was because she kept leaning against me, turning almost sideways so that her big breasts could move against my ribs.

"You'd better come in my car," I murmured.

"I think I'd better, too."

"We can come back for yours tomorrow."

I opened the Starfire door and helped her slide in on the bucket seat. Her tight gray skirt crept up to the middle of her stockinged thighs. Dori Pierce had good legs, and where her black nylons ended, I could see stretches of white thighs, wide and soft. The schoolteacherish look was gone, suddenly. Her black hair was loose, coming out of the tight bun to spread about her shoulders. When she saw me looking at her legs, she reached down and tugged at the thin nylon stocking, pulling it up higher on her thigh, tightening it and fixing the garter snap.

"I've never had one of her studs," she said softly.

My hand went to her knee and slid up and around her meaty thigh. The skin was warm. She gave a little gasp and brought her other thigh in so that she held my hand trapped. Her arms came around my neck and drew me down to her open mouth. Neither of us said a word. Our lips crushed together, our tongues touched and darted and I heard her breath working like a fireside bellows.

"Damn you, damn you," she whimpered after a while, "get in, get in. Ever since Bill, I vowed I'd never—but you're hers and anything of hers I can steal from her is—"

She pushed me away and sat huddled in the bucket seat, staring straight ahead. I closed the door gently, went around to the other side and got in. When the car was moving along Route 33, I started to probe at her with words.

"Who's Bill? Your husband? An old boy friend?"

"I was engaged to marry him six years ago. He—died."

"Why didn't you marry someone else?"

She was silent for two miles. Then she said, "Felicia Marr wouldn't let me." Her silken legs were close together now, drawn up almost into a foetal position against her chest. She sat with her arms wrapped around them, brooding straight ahead as though wondering where the road would take her.

"How could she stop you?"

"I'd rather not talk about it."

She turned her head, looked at me, chuckling. "I hate these console cars. They're a menace to romance. How in hell can a girl get chummy with her date in one of them?"

"You have a point there. Why don't we try and figure something out?" I was interested in romance with Dori Pierce only as a wedge with which to start her talking about her past. I felt I needed to know why she hated Felicia Marr, maybe even what sort of hold she had over Doc Vance, too.

If I could go to work on her for half an hour, she would talk. And she was just drunk enough to make the attempt interesting. I reached over and patted one of the knees she was gripping with her arms.

Suddenly she giggled and let her legs fall apart. "Problems. Everybody's got problems. See? It's too far to reach, all on account of the console between these seats."

"We could go in the back, but it's a little cramped for anything energetic. You can't even stretch out on the front seat because of the shift rod."

She turned on the red leather, kneeling so she faced me. "Maybe we could work it this way." She put her hands on the metal divider and leaned forward to jam her mouth on mine.

She blocked my vision, naturally. I slowed the car to a stop. She was breathing heavily again and so, to my vague surprise, was I. There was something about Dori Pierce—an intensity, a streak of sensuality deeply hidden—that made kissing her a hair-raising experience.

"Drive, damn you," she breathed into my mouth.

As if sensing that her head was in my way she lowered it to kiss my throat. Her fingers worked on my sport shirt, undoing buttons. I eased the car forward, got it up to thirty. I didn't dare drive faster because she was biting my chest, nibbling at it here and there, using her tongue on the skin.

After a while she whispered, "You belong to her. And I'm going to get you. I'm going to get you for a little while, at least." It was an eerie sensation, her busying herself with my body, me unable to do anything about it, and her voice chanting evil things in my ears.

I turned into the drive and let the Olds slide forward until it was in the garage. Then she moved back to her own bucket seat and waited. She was very quiet, but breathing so deeply her breasts trembled.

As I opened her door she put her hands on me. "We

can't go up to our rooms," she said harshly. "She might see us. You should have stopped along the way."

"She won't see us. She took sleeping pills."

"How do you know?"

I was pulling her out of the car and up against me, bending to kiss her moist lips. "Because we're playing golf tomorrow and she wants to be at her best."

"What about—oh! Yes, yes—get down to the skin!"

My hands were under her suit jacket, along her shirt-waist, searching through it for the snaps of her brassiere even as I kissed her soft throat. They came undone to my fingers and my chest felt her breasts loosen behind the lastex, surging against me. Her breathing sounded like two bellows now. I brought my hands around to her front.

Without undoing her blouse I shoved the brassiere down so that its cups formed supports for her breasts. Then my fingers hunted for and found her rigid nipples. I caught them, gripped them.

She shook all over, crying out.

"You really don't care whether Felicia finds us together or not, do you?" I asked her soft throat.

"No. Oh, God—no!"

"As a matter of fact, it would pay her back for all she's been doing to you these past six years."

"Oh, it would. It would!"

"Let's get out of here—somewhere comfortable."

She came willingly enough, stumbling beside me across the graveled area between the converted stables and the house. As moonlight touched her face, I saw her lower lip caught between her teeth and sweat beading her forehead. Between what the liquor was doing to her insides and what I had been doing to her outside, she was like a person hypnotized, ready for the mesmerist's command.

She tripped going up the back porch but I caught her and leaned her against the wall while I opened the door with my key. Then my arm was around her middle and we were sliding inside into the blackness and the quiet.

"You go up the stairs first," I told her, putting my hand on either side of her wide hips. "I'll come right behind you, to hold you."

It took us a few minutes to get to the top. She had to pause every so often to let her head clear, but when she did that I reminded her I was right behind her by slipping my hands under her gray skirt and stroking her nyloned legs and the bare thighs where the nylons ended.

She turned at the head of the stairs and put her arms around me, bringing my head against her middle. "I feel like screaming," she whispered into the darkness. "I would, too, except that it would bring—her."

"I thought you didn't care about Felicia Marr finding us."

"Nor do I—but I don't want to be found out before we climb into my bed." She laughed throatily above me, and the sound sent ripples of excitement down my spine.

My hands turned her, marched her forward.

We went into her room. From earlier in the night when I'd been in it, I remembered where the bed was. I brought her to it, made her sit down while I turned on a night-table lamp. It gave a rosy glow to the room.

Her eyes blinked at me. I drew in my breath slowly, seeing her black hair falling loose about her shoulders and the way her breasts shoved into her blouse. Through its thin linen I could make out large brown nipples standing stiffly.

I stood before her, reached to the blouse collar, caught hold of the material and ripped downward. Tiny pearl buttons flew as the linen tore. My hands gripped the blouse and brought it with her suit jacket down her back so that her arms were caught behind her and she was helpless, her arms gripped by the box jacket and her town shirtwaist.

I let her sink back on the bed and bent over her. She was crying out softly as my lips caressed her bared breasts, staring sightlessly up at the white ceiling. Her body shook under me, arching and falling back as her head moved left and right on the counterpane.

"Please—oh, God! Darling, please—"

"Bill used to do this to you, didn't he?"

"Yes, yes."

"Until Felicia came between you?"

"Not exactly."

"Tell me."

"You won't stop?"

"No, I won't stop."

She told me about herself between cries of ecstasy and pleas for me to keep on with what I was doing . . .

His name had been Bill Manners. He had been an accountant—a good one—making a big salary with Prince and Waters. Dori Pierce and Bill had been engaged to marry. During the summer they went to spend a weekend at Bill's cabin on Meadow Lake. Bill drove her to the cabin where he left her alone for a few hours while he went to make a call on a client.

She had seen a tramp during the long lonely afternoon, a rough-looking character who kept watching her from a distance. When she went for a swim off the boat landing he came along to stare at her. He laughed drunkenly when she threatened to call the state troopers' headquarters nearby, but he had gone away, promising to be back.

Terrified, she had waited for Bill to return.

It grew dark. She was afraid to light a lamp, but she had found a loaded revolver—Bill used it to shoot wild rabbits with—and sat waiting for his car headlights, the gun in her hands.

It grew to be nine o'clock, then ten. It was almost eleven when she heard the footsteps shuffling in the yard. Paralyzed, she tried to cry out, but could not. It was the tramp, she was sure. Tiptoeing to the door, she opened it a little. It was a dark night, but she could see a darker figure in the yard, standing motionless and looking at the house.

She lifted the gun, held it ready.

Her tongue was sticking to the roof of her mouth so she could not cry out, either in warning or for help. The place was lonely. There were no other cabins within miles.

The man standing there stirred, moved toward the house. She raised the gun, gripping it in both hands. She called out, "Stay where you are or I'll shoot."

All she heard was a chuckle.

The man came to the porch and up the steps. She had a vague glimpse of a floppy hat, baggy trousers and a heavy shirt.

She fired. The sound of the gun was an explosion in her ears. The man gave a gurgling cry, went back two steps and fell off the porch to the ground. Beyond him she saw the headlights of a car.

"Bill," she screamed. "Oh my God—Bill!"

She ran blindly past the motionless man and toward the road. The headlights picked her out and the car slowed. It was not Bill. Felicia Marr was in the car. At the time, she had not known her. She babbled about the tramp, how he had threatened to come back and how she was deathly afraid.

Felicia got out of the car and came back with her. Together they looked down at the man Dori thought was a tramp.

"Bill," Dori breathed and fainted.

She came to alongside Felicia Marr in her sports convertible. Somehow Felicia had dragged or carried her to her car, then had gone back inside the cabin to gather her things together, to bring her valise to her car trunk, to obliterate any evidence that Dori Pierce had been with Bill Manners that day.

"If you're smart, you'll forget you were ever in that cabin," Felicia advised. "I'm on my way to my own place, a dozen miles up the lake. I'll say you've been with me all the time. The police will find the body but they'll think a tramp shot him. Tramps have been breaking into these cabins all winter long. It won't be anything new. There have been other shootings here before now. You just keep a still tongue in your head."

The only trouble was, Felicia Marr had the gun with which Dori had shot her boy friend. She gave Dori a job as her private secretary—this was in the days after Felicia's father died and before she married Cletus Marr—and held the threat of exposure over her head.

She had been too paralyzed with shock to think clearly, at first; she had killed the man she loved, with her hand she had shot him down. She let Felicia do her thinking for her. When in the course of the routine police investigation she had been questioned—her picture and name and address had been in Bill Manner's wallet, naturally enough —Felicia said she'd been with her, that she had hired Dori Pierce and was bringing her up to her place, that she meant in the morning to drive her over to see Bill.

The coroner's jury had found that Bill Manners had been killed by a person or persons unknown, probably a tramp. They reconstructed the events leading up to his death by showing that he had visited a client and had remained there talking business until after dark. On the way back to his cottage, his car had broken down.

Two witnesses were found who had seen him working on it, getting his clothes dirty. Apparently he had given up the car as a bad job, had walked back to his lakeside house wearing his floppy old fishing hat, for some unknown reason. (Later, Dori thought he meant to play a joke on her, but the jest had backfired for Bill Manners.) Whatever the causes and the motives for his conduct, Dori Pierce was safe—thanks to Felicia Marr.

Dori went to work for Felicia. After a while, she began to do favors for her—because of the threat that Felicia

91

would expose her to the police—things like blackmailing men in high business circles. She would go naked to bed with these men and let a photographer snap pictures of her in certain erotic acts. The men would be rivals of Marr Enterprises, men who thought they were getting to Felicia Marr's private secretary. In one way they were, but they were always sorry for it afterwards.

Dori Pierce was in deep now.

Deep enough to kill . . .

I had her down to girdle and sheer black nylons by this time. My own clothes lay tossed across a chair. I had learned enough to understand both women a little better.

Felicia Marr had a strong compulsion to dominate everyone with whom she came in contact. Me. Dori Pierce. Probably Doctor Thurlow Vance, too, though I hadn't heard his story yet. She was like a slave owner. Her word must be obeyed, under penalty of punishment, perhaps even the death sentence. She wanted complete control over other human beings.

Dori Pierce, on the contrary, wanted only one thing.

A man.

She writhed and twisted against me, helping me get her out of her black girdle. We left the stockings on, since they added to her appeal. I drew her to me, let my hands and lips tell her body how much I needed her, how much she needed me. She gave bubbling cries as she thrust herself to me.

It was wild and savage between us.

I woke to sunlight in my eyes and lifted an arm to cover my face. The movement made me realize I was not in bed alone. Nor was I in my room. Moving up on an elbow, I stared down at Dori Pierce, at the long black hair trailing across her pillow like an ebony fan. Her face looked peaceful—like that of a child—and flushed with sleep.

I drew the covers up over her bare shoulders. She made a throaty sound and wriggled deeper into the mattress. One eye came open. Then she lifted her head and stared at me, eyes wide.

"Oh my God," she breathed.

I remembered Felicia Marr just as she was doing. I had a golf date with her. What in hell was the time? My Accutron said eleven minutes after eight. I threw back the covers. We were due on the tee at ten.

Dori watched me as I gathered up my clothes. At the door I turned and looked back at her where she lay with her arms clasped behind her head, bare arms rising out of the coverlets.

"Thank Felicia for me," she said lazily.

"Thank her? For what?"

"For the loan of her man." Her eyes were dark, slumberous, secretive. Then she smiled. "Don't mind me, David. I'm just being bitchy. You're a doll. It's too bad you're wasted on someone like her."

With a hand she blew me a kiss as I went out into the hall. I had to hurry. After a quick shower, I got into slacks, sport shirt and a warm sweater. I lifted my bag and clubs. I had made it in less than twenty minutes.

A good thing, too. I met Felicia coming down the small steps that connected our hallway with the new wing where she had her bedroom. She wore an almond-green pullover, a beige skirt, and light tan golf shoes on her feet. I took her bag from her shoulder and turned her back the way she had come. I didn't want her talking to Dori Pierce right then.

"I think I overslept," I told her matter-of-factly.

"Have any trouble with Dori?"

"She was too far gone to give anybody trouble."

She led the way into the kitchen where Elvira Bennett was making scrambled eggs with ham. The perking coffee smelled good. I found, as I sat down, that I was ravenous. I ate, studying this woman who held so many lives in the soft palms of her hands.

She looked younger this morning. Sleep had been a tonic to her body, hiding the tiny lines in her face so that all you noticed was the big red mouth and the purple eyes, the black hair like a frame for her lovely face. You could not see the underlying will to power that held Dori Pierce in thrall, or the secret—whatever it was—that could bring Thurlow Vance hotfooting it from an important operation to her bedside because she had a headache. This morning she was simply a stunningly groomed rich woman, and no more, as she sipped her coffee and let her eyes smile at me over the cup rim.

I wondered how the operation had turned out on the patient abandoned by Doc Vance.

"In the mood for a good game?" she asked.

"One of my best," I said nodding.

"Good. We tee off on the fourteenth at exactly ten."

"Off the fourteenth?"

"It's a new wrinkle Bram thought up. To save time, various foursomes go to the eighteen tees all over the course. At exactly ten the caddy master stands close to the tenth tee and fires a blank shell from a shotgun. It's like a starting signal. As soon as they hear it, everybody drives. For instance, we start at fourteen and end on thirteen.

"Instead of having only one group at a time moving out, we have all eighteen, or seventy-two golfers in all, in action at once."

"Well, great. Where does Bram start?"

"Where Bram wants. As golf champ, he's usually accorded the privilege of selecting his own group."

We took the Starfire to the country club.

I wondered as we drove if Felicia caught the scent of Dori Pierce's musky perfume that still clung to the bucket seat where she had knelt and kissed me while I drove her home. I cursed my stupidity in making a play for her. I became acutely aware that all it could cost me was an easy job—Dori Pierce could go to the electric chair.

Felicia said nothing, though I surprised a thoughtful look on her face. It might be that she was considering the coming game, however. I parked in the blacktopped lot alongside the clubhouse. It was fifteen minutes of ten. Just enough time for us to reach the fourteenth tee without hurrying.

I let Felicia lead the way. I carried the bags. When we came in sight of the little bench that flanked the tee, I saw a man and woman sitting there waiting for us.

I did not know the woman.

The man was Bram Skoronski.

NINE

HE WAS AS BIG as ever, and looking even broader in a heavy Shetland sweater. His face was bland as he smiled at Felicia, his big hand calling our attention to the woman still on the bench.

"Cele, you know Felicia. Her young man's name is David Mason Horne. He's an import from the South."

Celia Dawes smiled at me. She was an attractive redhead in a too-tight jersey that gripped her hips and breasts with revealing candor. I had the feeling she was more concerned with making an impression on her partner than she was with her golf game. Felicia had been at some pains to fill me in on her background as we'd driven over to the club, telling me she was number two girl on Bram Skoronski's eligibility list.

"Bram wants to get married. He's reached a point in his career where a wife can be a help to him, if only because she's a social asset."

I studied Celia Dawes without seeming to do so. She was a dress designer, a girl whose creations stressed the person who wore the dress rather than the garment itself. A Dawes gown was both a work of art and a personal ornament for a woman, according to Felicia. Her business was worth close to a million dollars and was getting bigger every day. For her, Bram Skoronski would be quite a catch. And she was grimly determined to snare him.

Deceptively sweet to Felicia, she ignored me. I could imagine what Bram had told her about David Mason Horne, hired escort. She won the toss and addressed her ball with a seductive wiggle of her hips, knowing Bram was watching.

Her drive was a good one, a hundred and eighty yards straight down the fairway. Felicia hit for a little over one-fifty. Bram hammered out a real longie, two-forty at least. I drove last.

The power of a golfer, like that of a hitter in baseball, is mainly in the wrists. Bram Skoronski was bigger, heavier and more muscular that I, but I had thick, strong wrists. I swung and watched my ball soar. It went to within ten feet of Bram's Teebird. I was satisfied.

The fourteenth hole was a long one that skirted a woods to the left and a row of new summer cottages to the right. If you left the fairway you were in trouble. As we walked I told Felicia to forget distance for accuracy. The hole was a long one, over six hundred yards, and she looked troubled.

"I always get a seven on this one. Or worse."

"If you're on the green in four, one putt will even you out at par. Try for it."

She sighed, but agreed. She used a wood for her second shot and slammed her Spalding more than halfway to the green. Cele tried for distance and hooked into the rough. I could hear Bram muttering under his breath. I gathered from his tone that nothing mattered so much to him as coming out on top today.

Felicia was on in four and took two putts for a six. Cele

had a seven. Bram and I were par. We had a one stroke advantage moving onto the fifteenth tee.

We played evenly through to the eighteenth hole where Cele topped her drive. Her ball rolled twenty feet and stopped. Bram swore audibly. His dark mood worsened when Felicia rammed a sweet one, but close to one-ninety. I went next and hit mine two-thirty, maybe closer to two-forty, straight down the fairway. Bram felt that his team's chance depended solely on his efforts. He took a long time addressing the ball. Too long. It gave him time to think.

He sliced into the rough and needed two to get back.

We left the eighteenth hole with a three-up lead.

Felicia sang as she walked along, though she was quiet enough on the tees or the greens. Impish laughter lay in her purple eyes, and from time to time she would throw her arms high over her head in an excess of good spirits. Whenever she did this, Celia Dawes gritted her teeth and pouted.

Finally Bram told her to shut up. Felicia looked innocent but inwardly she was convulsed. The great Bram Skoronski was going to pieces right before her eyes. The Long Hills golf champion was coming apart at the seams.

On the third tee, Bram pulled himself together. The man could play golf, I give him that; he put Cele and Felicia and me out of his mind and concentrated on his game. Our three-stroke lead dwindled to two, then one.

On the tenth hole he came up with an eagle, two under par. Since the rest of us hit for par, that put Cele and Bram one stroke in the lead. Felicia looked at me and shrugged. She was saying, in effect, *It was fun while it lasted but I really didn't expect to win.*

I had expected to win, however. I still did.

We had three holes left in which to catch and beat them. The eleventh was a water hole, a hundred and seventy yards to the green, which made a level plateau with sloping sand traps on every side but the front, where the neatly cropped grass ran down to a small pond.

To play the hole safe, you dropped your ball as close to the edge of the pond as you dared. The others played it that way. I decided to go over it. If I made it, we stood to win the hole and even the score. I refused to think about failing.

Felicia and Cele were about thirty feet from the pond, in nice position to pitch over it onto the green. I drove next with a five iron. My ball lofted and dropped and my heart sank with it. Too short, just a bit too short. It would hit the slope and bounce, but not hard enough to make the green. Its momentum would carry it back into the water.

I heard Bram chuckle and say, "Too bad, sport."

Then Felicia cried out. There must have been a pebble where the Maxfli landed because the ball ricocheted upward—too fast and too hard for it to have landed in dirt—and cleared the rim of the green. It plunked down on velvety grass carpeting and rolled straight for the lip of the hole. It came to rest less than a foot from the pin.

I was lucky. My slamming heart told me so, as did Bram Skoronski when he turned and glared. Cele gave a little shrug and laughed. Felicia hugged herself. Bram drove last. It was up to him to overcome my advantage. He had a clear choice: play safe this side of the pond or go over it. He chose to go over, as I had.

He hit it too far. The ball sailed above the green and beyond it into the bunker. Felicia laughed. I think Bram would have hit her if Celia hadn't seen the look on his face and stepped between them.

Felicia watched them walk off the tee with flushed face and brilliant eyes. Anger was deep inside her. She was trembling when my hand touched her arm.

"If he'd dared! If he'd ever dared!" she breathed.

"Easy, easy. Don't get emotional at this late date."

Her purple eyes slid sideways at me. "It might ruin things, mightn't it? I mean, right now we're in a good spot to take the marbles."

"To beat Bram Skoronski, at any rate," I amended.

She gestured. "Same thing. Bram always wins the spring tourney. It's become a habit." We walked along for a score of yards before she said, "This means a lot to me now. If we beat Bram—I don't give a good goddamn about the tourney itself—I'll put a five-thousand-dollar check in your hand when we go home."

I grinned, "Honey, you've just lost money."

Felicia smiled tightly. "Say I've won my pride back."

She and Cele were on the green in two and took one putt apiece to par. Bram had lost his temper completely by this time. He used three to get out of the sand, three more to hole out. I sank my putt for a birdie two.

We were ahead by five, with two holes to play.

It ended that way, with Felicia posting a very creditable seventy-nine, Cele a seventy-eight, Bram Skoronski a seventy-four. I had a sixty-eight. It was good to see our

97

one-forty-seven hit the bulletin board. Felicia was pleased as hell. She decided to stick around for the fun.

"We'll have a cocktail and lunch in the restaurant, just as we are. The other scores will be coming in fast now. I want to see if Bram is man enough to congratulate us."

We had martinis, and steak sandwiches with coffee.

By the time we were done, we heard the news that we were number one team, the winners of the silver cup, and that the Skoronski-Dawes duo had placed third. The club president came over to congratulate us, as did most of the other contestants, Cele Dawes with them.

Bram Skoronski had gone home, Cele told us, "I thought he'd burst a blood vessel on the eleventh," she smiled ruefully. "That or clobber you, Lise."

"It was mean of me to laugh," Felicia nodded.

"But human," Cele murmured, patting her hand.

For the first time, the redhead looked at me. "Maybe I can get you as a partner when Felicia makes up with Bram, David. I'd like to get my name on that cup before I get so old it doesn't matter."

"Sure thing," I nodded.

Felicia did not speak but her eyes were thoughtful.

On the way back to her place she said, "David, business will keep me up to my neck for the next three weeks or a month. After that I want to go to Europe."

"And?"

Her fingertip moved along her skirted thigh, up and down. "I want you to make all the arrangements—places to see, reservations, schedules, things like that. You can operate from an office in my building."

I turned my head and looked at her. A trip to Europe doesn't require anybody to spend five days a week, for a month, to get things ready. Felicia Marr wanted me out of Westport, away from the country club. And from Dori Pierce?

"Whatever you say. You're the boss," I told her.

"Yes," she breathed out slowly. "I am the boss. Your boss, the only boss. Don't ever forget·it. I can play rough if I need to."

The check for five thousand dollars she gave me just before dinner took some of the sting out of her words. Dori Pierce had gone into the city to stay at a hotel for a while. I wanted to ask Felicia if the move had been made at her order. I decided not to.

There is a saying about sleeping dogs.

Daily I drove into the city with Felicia Marr. We used the Starfire and I parked it in the garage in her building. She paid a regular monthly fee for the privilege. I was given a room with a desk, a chair and a telephone in it. I needed nothing more for the work I did.

The new *S.S. France* was the ship I chose for our trip. An eighty-million-dollar ocean liner, she was the last word in luxury living on the high seas. Her two pools, her theater, her modernistically decorated bar and smoker promised fun and games for the four days plus it would take to dock at Le Havre.

I planned our itinerary carefully, with an eye to what Felicia would like most to see. From Le Havre we would go by plane to Paris. There we would make the Ritz our headquarters, while we visited the Louvre and the Tuileries during the daytime hours, with time left over in which to walk around Les Halles, the great marketplace where you can buy anything man can eat. Our nights would be devoted to pleasure, at the Mayol, where they put us on one of the spicier girlie shows, the Folies Bergére, the intimate Comédie de Paris and the Moulin Rouge in the Pigalle section, the more expensive Lido, the Naturists, and of course the Crazy Horse saloon.

Felicia would want to visit the fashion salons, the House of Patou, of Bagardoy, of Lentheric for perfumes, and many of the shops along the Rue de Rivoli. I made a schedule for her to go by, including a boat trip down the Seine for both of us, with a visit afterwards to the famed La Mère Catherine restaurant. A little more than a week would do for Paris.

I wanted to get into Germany to visit the Intermezzo in Munich, then spend a day or two in Hamburg so I could show her around the Reeperbahn. She had to have a stomach for this latter street; it bore the reputation of the most wicked in the world; anything you wanted in the way of sexual pleasure you could buy there if you had the money to spend.

Denmark was to be our next port of call. Felicia would want to see Copenhagen—a great European shopping center—since she was so much the businesswoman. We would visit Tivoli Park and eat in the Belle Terrasse under trellised arbors. I decided that Danish silver and the world-renowned porcelains might tempt her purse. After this, we would sip Cherry Heering at the plant where it was made.

It is easy to write all this. It was not so easy to pick and choose, to put by a visit to Norway to see the famous Vigeland statues in Oslo, or the beaches in Sweden where men and women swim nude together and nothing is thought of it. Finland and Scandinavia would have to wait their turns. I would have liked her to see the Swiss Alps, the Acropolis at sunrise, a bullfight in the arena at Madrid. These, too, would have to be postponed.

For I wanted most of all to show Felicia Italy, with its blue grottos, its tiny fishing villages, its limpid waters and sunny skies. There is no land like Italy for romance. If I had my way, she would rent a villa—overlooking Capri, perhaps—and spend a year or two just enjoying life. I had to allow two weeks at least for Florence, Milan and the coast around Capri. I would have liked it to be longer.

Felicia was delighted with my schedule, especially when she discovered I intended to stop over in London for a long weekend and come home by PanAm jet. This was to be a combination business and pleasure jaunt for her. She had certain contacts in Italy—she wanted to make some sort of deal with Emilio Pucci who designs expensive sportswear as well as evening gowns and exquisite scarves—and arrange for the opening of a branch office in Rome. In London she was interested in opening a smart shoppe for American tourists at the airport.

She told me all this sitting in front of her vanity mirror in an open housecoat under which she was stark naked. From time to time as she turned animatedly, this way and that, I caught sight of a full breast with its swollen brown nipple trembling gently. It was a little over a week since my night with Dori Pierce. Felicia had seemed uninterested in me physically; I had supposed that affairs at the office were exhausting her. Now I was not so sure.

She stood up and let the brocade garment slip from her shoulders to her waist, turning to study her reflection in the glass. Her body was that of a young woman. Her flesh was white and smooth, her belly gently mounded. Looking at her you would have said she was less than thirty. Until she got that cold look around the eyes; then you knew her for what she was, an older woman with a strange compulsion, a little afraid of growing old and finding herself undesirable.

I went to her, bent to run my mouth along her shoulder. She pressed back against me, moving her hips from side to side and laughing deep in her throat.

"Poor darling! Do I get you so excited?"

100

"What do you think?"

"I think I do and—it's too bad."

"Is it?"

She caught my hands that reached for her breasts, put them down by my sides, still watching her reflection through half-closed eyes. She was Lorelei, standing naked with her housecoat held to her hips only because they pressed into my loins. An older Lorelei, with nothing on her mind but herself.

"I've been working like a truck horse, David. You know that. I don't have any energy left over for this sort of thing."

She knew how I felt, well enough. I thought maybe she wanted me to beg. Damned if I would! If she got her kicks out of teasing me, let her. Felicia sighed and stepped away. The housecoat fell between us. In her bedroom slippers she pattered naked to her closet, full white buttocks shaking to her every step. The bitch. The teaser. Maybe I should have looked away but my eyes were magnetized to her nudity.

She let me watch as she slipped a pink nightgown over her head. In it, she might as well have remained naked. She walked back toward me, smiling faintly, knowing she tortured me. Was it because of Dori Pierce? Did she want me to see what she had to offer and—would not?

She put her bare arms around my neck. "Kiss me good-night, dearest. Then get a good rest."

I needed a rest the way I needed a slit throat but she was getting a charge out of me, so I let her enjoy herself. What else could I do? She was paying me two hundred a week; it was the least I could do for her. She wanted to tease me to distraction, so I let her.

I even added to my own discomfort by putting my palms on her soft buttocks and bringing her hips closer. Laughter gurgled on her lips when I did that. She rested her cheek against mine and whispered that when we were on the *France*, she would be ever so loving. She would reward me then for being so patient now.

"Sure," I said. "You bet."

I was about to close her bedroom door—she was in bed with the covers pulled up to her navel—when she said sweetly, "It's too bad Dori's in town, isn't it?" Her fingers wriggled at me. I wondered if my face showed how cold I felt.

I said, "What's Dori got to do with us?"

101

"The other night when you brought her home, you stayed with her in her room." She said it matter-of-factly, but by this time I had come to know Felicia Marr. Inside, she was blazing hot with anger. You could have torn her skin with red pincers, however, before she would show it.

"You're nuts," I said inelegantly. "I put her to bed, I turned on her night-table light—and I left her. You think differently—you're wrong."

Her eyelids flickered. Her tongue came out to moisten her lips. "I saw her light on. It was on all night." Her voice sounded oddly like that of a little girl, puzzled and a little frightened.

"So maybe she left it on. I wouldn't know."

"Your light never went on," she murmured.

"Hell! I was tired. Have you ever gotten out of bed around one o'clock and had to go looking for some drunken dame who couldn't stand up?" I let my anger come into my face and voice. This rich bitch was trying to run lives. She wouldn't bed me but nobody else could, either. *The hell with you, honey. Dori Pierce gave me a better time than you ever have! Maybe because she's a woman and not a bundle of neuroses.* Her face showed surprise at my fury, and the faint beginning of doubt began to show.

"I was so sure—"

"Why didn't you come in and catch us in the act?"

·I knew damn well why: she was afraid. Dori Pierce was years younger than she, and that fear of age which lives in every woman was especially active in Felicia Marr. If she had confirmed her suspicions, she would have had to let me go, and I was too much fun to boss around and to tease, to give me up so easily. It was better this way, suspecting but not knowing for sure.

I did just what she hoped I'd do. I went out and slammed the door behind me—but I let her voice coax me back as she stood in the open doorway with the bedroom light making her nightgown disappear like mist before a morning sun.

"Don't go to bed angry, darling," she whispered.

"I guess you think I have no feelings."

"I'm sorry, honestly. I am. But I was so sure."

"Well, now you know."

"Kiss me and make up."

We kissed and made up. Then she closed the door in my face. I stood there breathing harshly, my nostrils filled with her fragrance, my palms remembering the softness of her flesh under her Odette Barsa nightgown. I would take a long time to fall asleep, I realized.

The days went like cold molasses flowing uphill.

Every morning I drove Felicia to work and spent the day doodling at my desk. I saw Dori Pierce from time to time, moving about busily; once I invited her out to lunch. She looked scared and I gathered that Felicia had made a few warning sounds.

I always ate alone. Felicia had business lunches and conferences to keep her busy. A hundred times a day I checked over our reservations, our tickets. Europe took on the aspects of a Nirvana in my eyes. There I would set the pace, lay down the rules. I would be guide and lover at the same time—or so, at least, I believed.

As though she wanted to drive me frantic with desire for her body, Felicia always summoned me into her bedroom when she wanted to discuss the trip. No other place would do. She would be in tight toreadors and naked from her navel upward except for a string of beads. I had to talk about the *S.S. France* and our stateroom while standing before her vanity mirror, wondering how many brassieres she would bring with her.

Or she might be wearing a brassiere and girdle with sleek nylons on her legs. At those times she'd ask if I thought she should shop for underwear in Paris or in Rome, and should she take the bare minimum of clothing with her? And what about bathing suits? Would she need to bring a bikini or would it be more fun to wear those abbreviated things they wore at St. Topitz? She made me sit and watch her, all the time knowing she was not available. It grew into a game between us.

I had never known a woman with so many varieties of revealing garments. It had become a fetish with her. Once she informed me that a particular pair of panties had been purchased as part of her wedding trousseau for Fred Ostringer. A peek-a-boo brassiere through which her brown nipples protruded was bought with her second husband, the count, in mind. She put them on while I watched, and paraded around the room in them for me.

She never let me touch her. I could sit on the bed and admire her all I wanted but it was a hands-off proposition, all the way. I suppose she thought she was demonstrating her power over me. She was, all right—until I just about went crazy.

103

One night when she had on a black lace set of pajamas through which I could see every color tint and flesh tone of her body, I'd had enough teasing. I grabbed her and pulled her down on the bed, covering her lips with mine while I ripped the taunting lace jacket and lace pants off her body. I would have raped her, I guess, except that she screamed and clawed like a terrified virgin. She bit my neck until the blood ran and her fingernails made twin furrows on my cheeks.

She squirmed out from under me and ran to her night table. From its drawer she drew a gun and aimed it at my middle. Her eyes were pools of rage, of humiliated pride. She drove my desire away for fair. I thought sure she was going to send a bullet into my belly.

"You leching bastard," she rasped. "I ought to shoot you where it will hurt the most."

"All right, all right," I soothed her. "Take it easy. I made a mistake." I was talking fast because I was looking into her eyes and not liking what I saw. She was a madwoman at that moment. "Look, I promise. It won't happen again, Felicia. For God's sake, put the gun down."

"I'll kill you if you attack me again. I swear to God I will! I won't be manhandled. I won't be taken like a plaything, like some girl you might pick up off the streets."

"Of course not," I agreed, keeping my hands up and palms out. I was shaking, watching that gun barrel. It didn't quiver in the slightest. It was aimed right at me. The slightest jar, the least pressure of her finger, and it would explode.

It was a near thing. She was so absolutely insane with rage her body trembled in the remnants of the black lace pajamas as though with ague. If I hadn't been so terrified I might have appreciated the picture she made. *Outraged Innocence* could have been its title. Or *Virtue Defending Itself*. At the moment, all I could think about was staying alive.

"I said I was sorry," I went on. "You don't realize how exciting you are. You've been teasing me for the past couple of weeks, almost every night, until I'm just about ready to climb walls. I'm flesh and blood, Felicia. Not wood. I have feelings."

She considered that while she kept the deadly little Walthian Beretta trained on me. She liked what she heard about herself, especially the bit about her being an exciting woman. In a sense, what I had done made her out as

104

irresistible. No woman can ignore that kind of compliment, even a woman like Felicia Marr.

The gun lowered. She smiled faintly and looked down at herself. The black lace jacket trailed in shreds from her shoulders; the black lace trousers hung around her knees.

"I suppose I'll have to forgive you. I didn't realize I was having such an effect on you, David."

Like hell you didn't, you bitch!

The gun went into the drawer. Her hand closed the drawer. She shrugged out of the jacket and let the trousers drop to the rug. "There goes three hundred dollars," she said, stretching. She stood naked in front of me. "It isn't the money I care about, though. You understand that?"

I nodded, unable to speak. Amusement had replaced the fury in her eyes. She was having fun again. She came over and sat beside me, patting my wrist. "It will be different on the boat, I promise you that." She examined my cuts and bruises, taking her own sweet time about it so I would be sure to get uncomfortable again with her so close to me—and without a stitch on.

"You'd better get Elvira to put something on your cheeks. I gouged pretty deep, I'm afraid. Do they hurt?"

"A little. I'll live, I guess."

"Well, you'd better! We have a trip to take."

She kissed me and pushed me out the door. I went downstairs to hunt up Elvira Bennett and her first-aid kit. I was seething with suppressed fury. I needed to lash out at something, at someone.

I forgot my troubles when I heard a woman crying.

The crying stopped when I knocked at her door. Elvira came to open it, wiping her eyes. When she saw my face, she stared in horror.

"What happened to you?"

"Felicia happened to me. I made a pass at her when she didn't want me to. She did this. She thought you could patch me up."

"Come in."

I sat on a straight-backed chair while she fussed over me with salve and Band-Aids. The aftermath of her grief was still in her. I could hear her sobbing softly from the bathroom as she rummaged in her medicine cabinet.

"You don't look so chipper yourself," I said as she applied the iodine to my cuts. "What's bugging you?"

"The same thing that scratched you. Felicia Marr."

105

"What's she done now?"

"She did it a long time ago. I only learned recently. Last night, when I went out to dinner with Doctor Vance."

I remembered then that Felicia and I had eaten in the city, that it had been Elvira's day off. I could tell she wanted to talk, to unburden herself, so I led her with casual questions until I had the whole story.

"I told you the first day you arrived," she began nervously, putting the Band-Aid box back into her metal kit, "that I used to go around with Thurlow—Doctor Vance, that is—when we were in school. He married and I lost track of him for a while. Then his wife died. When Felicia Marr bought this house, I began seeing him again."

She had thought at first that he loved her and wanted to marry her, the way he acted, so sweet and all. He was so attentive and thoughtful she began smelling orange blossoms. They went out to dinner twice a week—their favorite spots were the Red Barn and the Carriage Drive—and spent her day off together, from early in the morning. They managed to see a movie or a show one night a week. They grew to be a habit with one another.

As the weeks and the months went by, she grew doubtful. Maybe marriage was something he wanted to avoid, having buried his first wife. She was never sure just where she stood with him. Oh, he was exciting enough, being only in his early forties and still a vigorous and healthy man.

She flushed a little when she told me how they used to stop at motels occasionally and spend the night. She had been a virgin but she had come to him with a hidden sensuality that made no bones about the fact that she wanted him—with or without marriage, though that was always in the back of her mind.

"Last night I had it out with him," she whispered.

She was sitting on the bed, staring down at her hands, flushing. Everyone has his limit; she had been pushed to hers. "I mentioned it to him, told him we weren't getting any younger."

"What did he say?"

"Said he couldn't marry me, that it wouldn't be fair. He says he wants to marry me, it's all he thinks of—but he can't."

"Why not?"

"Felicia Marr won't let him."

"How can she stop him?"

Twelve years ago, Thurlow Vance performed an abortion on a young girl and the girl had died. It was the first and only abortion he had ever done, and he did it only because the girl was the daughter of his best friend and had gotten into trouble. Something had gone wrong. In a proper hospital he might have saved her—in his own little office he could do nothing.

"How did Felicia learn about it?"

"The father worked for her. She guessed something was wrong, took him out and got him drunk, sympathized with him, wormed the story out of him. She even had him sign an affidavit. Then she sent him and his family to the West Coast office, where they are now.

"She didn't stop there. She hunted up the nurse who assisted at the operation, and paid her money to get her to sign an affidavit, too. Then she went to see Thurlow. She showed him photostats of the affidavits, told him he was her physician from then on, that if he behaved himself he could continue his prosperous practice, that she would forget what had happened. But he had to be always at her beck and call."

I remembered the night he had come over from the hospital just to cure her headache. I said, "She likes to play god."

"A god can't die. She can," whispered Elvira Bennett.

Dori Pierce had said some such thing, too.

Elvira smiled wistfully. "I was feeling blue. I just lay on my bed and cried and cried, until you knocked. I feel better now, more sensible. Things will work out somehow."

Calculation came into her eyes. "If she should have an accident over there in Europe—it would make a lot of people happy."

"I suppose it would. But I'm no murderer."

"No, you haven't got the guts."

She gasped a moment after she said it and looked sick. I smiled and shook my head. "Maybe you're right. Maybe I don't. Or maybe I have no reason to kill her. I think murder comes down to that, a good reason to commit it. For a sane person, that is."

I stood up and went to the door. She was still sitting on the bed, staring down at her hands. They were strong hands, like talons. She curved them as if she was seeing Felicia Marr's soft white throat in their grip.

Elvira Bennett had a reason to do murder.

As did Dori Pierce.

And Doctor Vance.

TEN

HER OFFICE THREW Felicia a big cocktail party in her stateroom on the *S. S. France*. I think half the staff was there—certainly all the more important people were. It was a catered affair, paid for by the executives—who drank the most Scotch and pinched the most behinds—with no expenses spared. The women received orchids, the men as much or as little as they wanted to drink. I sat in a corner during the whole affair, nursing a bourbon and water, and watched Felicia Marr.

She was a dozen women during the party. Her laughter rang out with brittle, shallow delight when she saw a friend and raised her arm in greeting. She was sober with three potbellied men in expensive Brooks Brothers suits, who were hemming her in to talk over the advisability of opening the London shop. She wept with a young girl because her boy friend had run off and married somebody else— and was angry at a steward who tried to keep the party at a reasonable decibel level.

Twice she came over to me, once to pat my cheek, and tell me not to mind her friends, that she collected well-wishers the way some people collect stamps or butterflies; the second time to bring me a drink, and to tell me not to be such a goddamn killjoy, to get out and mingle. An hour and a half, and nine or ten martinis, elapsed between visits. I missed count after a while, so there could have been more.

This was Felicia with her hair down—drunk. A Felicia Marr I had never seen. I found her fascinating. She kissed men, one arm around their necks, her free hand holding a cocktail glass. She let their hands move over her body without reproof, laughing shrilly and hugging them. I could take only so much of it. After a while I got up and walked out into the corridor and up the staircase to the promenade deck.

I let the salt air off the harbor blow at me as the noise died out. I thought about Doctor Vance and Elvira Bennett, about Dori Pierce and her periods of drunkenness. I wondered what this trip to Europe would mean to me.

There is a circumscribed routine to life on an ocean liner. You and your fellow passengers do things together, almost at the same time. You breakfast, walk the promenade deck, use the first-class pool, lunch, nap or play bridge, enjoy tea, then dress for dinner. After dinner there is the theater, of course; or more bridge; or, if you prefer, dancing in the salon.

I thought Felicia might have one of her tantrums because I walked out on her party, but instead, she complimented me on my good sense. She was an entirely different person when business was involved, she explained; I understood then that she had been aware of my staring at her. Actually, she went on—putting earrings to her lobes as I waited for her to go to dinner our first night out—it was all of a pattern.

She wanted power. She would do anything to get it, to hold it. Her palm patted my cheek as she walked past me to her jewelry box. "I can't stand to lose what I want as my own, darling. Always remember that, please. It will make things so much easier between us."

I told myself to remember it. I had no reason not to, not at the salary she was paying me. I earned my salary by setting out a schedule to keep her active, happy, forgetting business cares and her coming meetings in Rome and London. I laid out the schedule but I presented my ideas as mere suggestions, so that the decisions would come from her. I had learned she could not stand for anyone telling her what to do. The dictums in her life, even the minor ones, must be her own.

We played bridge after dinner, while the *France* moved her gigantic bulk—she is the longest liner afloat, with eleven decks—eastward from New York Harbor and the Statue of Liberty, heading into open sea. Felicia was an excellent player, I found. We complemented one another— she was a cautious bidder, I was reckless and inclined to gamble. I forced her up to slams several times, and she made them handily. We won over twenty dollars, even at the low stakes for which we played.

We had cocktails in the smoker before retiring.

To my surprise, I slept alone. I had been sure Felicia would want to forget her tensions in bed our first night out. I know I did. Maybe she suspected my own need and took this way of showing her authority. I wished Dori Pierce had been along. I would have gone to her cabin, and the hell with Felicia Marr.

We spent next morning on the sundeck, cooking. From time to time we went into the first-class pool, which is not as large as the tourist pool, surprisingly enough. Sun and water and wind, these were our companions for the first two days of our voyage. At night we played bridge, drank cocktails, and went to bed—separately. It was a relaxing, calming sort of program. It worked fine for Felicia Marr. Me, it damn near got in trouble.

There was a pretty model who went swimming the same time we did, and who was addicted to wearing bikinis of varying degrees of scantiness. She was a French girl who had come to the United States as part of a United Nations affair. Her name was Babette Famieux. She was petite, pretty, and looking for a shipboard romance. When we played together in the water while Felicia was sunning on the afterdeck, she rubbed against me, making sure I felt her hard little breasts and the softness of her taut buttocks. After seeing Felicia Marr in her own varying stages of undress for the past few weeks, night after night, I was as ripe for loving as a stud stallion.

Babette sensed that I was overdue for fun and games. Her eyes would glint with mischief whenever we were with Felicia. She would look at her, then at me, and get a funny little smile on her lips.

Sometimes she would whisper so only I would hear, " 'Ow would you like something younger, Daveed?"

Or she would be lying stretched out beside me on the rim of the pool in a more revealing bikini than ever, and say conversationally, "Is she really good, the old one?" Then she would sit up so I could see her taut belly and the upper slopes of her buttocks where the pantie part of her suit exposed them, and arch her eyebrows inquiringly, asking me to make comparisons.

On our third afternoon out, Felicia told me she would be shut up in her stateroom that night, and was giving me time off. She must go over certain papers related to her coming transactions in Rome and London, she said, wanting to mull them over in her mind before meeting her representatives.

I took her at her word.

Just before we came out of the pool I invited Babette to go dancing that night, just she and I. There would be cocktails, as many or as few as she wanted. Afterward, we would look at the moon from the promenade deck.

Laughter lurked in her eyes. "*Oui*—and after that?"

"The rest is up to you."

Babette wore a black satin dress that hugged her lithe young body when we met after dinner. As soon as I put my

110

arm about her middle for our first dance, I realized the dress was all she had on, the dress and high-heeled evening slippers.

She came to the tug of my arm willingly, letting her body caress me as we moved in the intricate steps of a samba. There was a musky perfume about her and a breathlessness just as stirring as her soft flesh. We moved in an aura of gin, absinthe, slow music and sensual anticipation. This would be our night, our chance to spill a libation to Eros.

Neither of us was in any hurry. We had the entire evening. Babette let her thighs stroke me in the dance, while I caressed her naked back and the curves of her buttocks every time we found ourselves in a shadowy corner. She let me guide her up a slow spiral of pleasure, nestling her head on my chest while her satin hips moved with subtle insinuation against my loins. Whenever the dance called for it, she came to me so that I could understand that her breasts were swollen in desire.

"Soon, *mon chéri,*" she whispered once, trembling. "Soon, soon."

Around eleven, I held her light evening wrap so she could slip it about her shoulders, then escorted her out onto the deck. A silver moon made a pale reflection on the smooth sea. It was a night for romance. I drew her to me at the rail, put my arms about her and kissed her.

Her lips were moist, sweet. There was a hunger in their curves that yawned to my tongue even as my hands moved under her wrap and onto the satin where it was most taut with her flesh. I let my fingers caress her stiff nipples, the outward bulge of her hips, and grew more aware of the need she had for me.

The *soon* became the *now* for Babette and me.

We walked from the rail, our arms about one another, her head tilted to my chest. The night was a throbbing hunger in me, reaching out through the darkness toward her softness, her warmth. In Babette I would find peace, a momentary happiness.

She gurgled French words in her throat, words I might have understood if I could have heard them; but she spoke them so low, so softly, that they were only a little whimper of sound telling me she felt just as I did. In such a way do the young make love, coating their need with a fantasy of romance, a willingness to believe that theirs was a moment unique in time and space.

Not for us the frenzied haste of older people, who come to love with the realization that time is so important. As it rushes by it must be caught and held with zealous fingers lest it slip away before they may drink of its intoxicating moments, savor its varied nuances, its every joy.

In a companionway I turned her, kissed her again.

We clung, caressing one another with gentle hands, slowly, lazily. It had been so long since I walked like this with a girl my own age, I had forgotten this sweetness, this tenderness.

A polite cough drew us apart.

A steward stood before us, his face like a mask. He told me I was wanted in the Marr stateroom—at once. I gathered that he had been looking all over for me.

"All right, I'll be along," I told him.

Babette waited until he was gone before taking a scented handkerchief from her handbag and rubbing the lipstick off my mouth. "I weel wait for you in my cabeen, Daveed. Do not be long, *s'il vous plaît*."

"She probably wants her warm milk," I rasped.

A shadow touched her face. Was that sadness in her eyes? A resignation to fate? A bittersweetness of lost opportunity which only the young know in all its poignant sorrow? I kissed the tip of her nose.

"Be with you in a jiffy," I promised.

Felicia was sitting at the little writing table when I entered. She took off her glasses and turned to me, hiding something on the desk with her elbow.

"Did you have a good time with your little French girl, David?" she asked brightly. Too brightly.

"What do you want? The steward said—"

Her ringed hand gestured airily. "Oh, the steward. I've had him watching you all evening, to report back to me what you were doing." The smile was tight, cold. "I thought it time to interfere before you committed some—folly."

"Interfere?" I asked dumbly.

"Why, yes. It isn't fair to your pretty trollop to let her get ideas about you, now is it? You belong to me."

My face must have expressed my gathering anger, for she said more sharply, "Don't you, David? Don't you belong to me?"

"Not entirely. I work for you, for a salary. No more." It was on the tip of my tongue to tell her I had not shot anyone as Dori Pierce had, nor had I aborted a young girl who later died, as had Doctor Vance. Her only hold on me was money.

I put my hand on the cabin doorknob. Almost shrilly she cried out, "Where are you going? Take your hand off that knob!"

"I'm going back to my trollop, as you call her. She's waiting for me." I locked stares with her, saw the savage fury deep inside her eyes. I added, "She doesn't treat me like a dumb thing without any feelings."

"How does she treat you, David?"

I felt the weeks of subjection to this woman, to her whims and teasings, gather in me like a storm cloud. "Like a human being. If she lets me kiss her or caress her, it's only because she wants me with her body. Oh, hell—I'm not naïve enough to think she's the love of my life, anything like that. She's a woman who wants me as a man, not as some sort of whipping boy."

Felicia said coldly, "You will stay the night with me."

"Not this night, I won't," I told her.

Her head tilted sideways as her purple eyes considered me. "You will stay or something very terrible will happen to you before you get back home. And possibly to your French girl."

My middle went cold. I was not afraid for myself, but Babette—there were men in Paris where she lived who would do anything for money, especially for the kind of money Felicia Marr could pay them—not a hundred or five hundred dollars but money running into the thousands. I wouldn't put it past her to have Babette killed in such a way that the French police might think me the guilty party. My guts were so tight they hurt.

I had opened the cabin door slightly. I pushed it shut and turned to stand with my back to it. "You would, too. You'd do anything to show your power over me."

"Yes, I would," she agreed.

She was sitting on the edge of the chair, stockinged knees together, her hands clasped into fists resting on her thighs. She wore a sequin sheath that was a Scassi original. It left her shoulders and the upper swells of her breasts bare and hugged her hips tightly. It was a new gown. I had never seen it before.

She stood up, holding her chin high.

"Undress me, David."

Babette Famieux was waiting for me in her stateroom. If I stayed with Felicia Marr, the little French girl would

113

hate me. Every part of me wanted to open the door and plunge out into the corridor, to escape from this woman standing in her evening gown with her bare arms by her sides. I wanted Babette, her youth, her firm young body. I wanted to dream with her as I made love to her, dream those dreams which only the young can share.

"On the writing desk, David," Felicia said.

I looked. There was a check there which her elbow had covered as she turned when I came into the room. Money. A thousand? Two thousand? I walked to the writing desk and looked down. The check was for ten thousand dollars.

"No girl in the world is worth that kind of money," Felicia said softly. She was still waiting there with her arms by her sides. I moved toward her, put my fingers on her zipper and ran it gently down her back.

Only soft flesh met my gaze. She had on no brassiere under the gown; one had been built into the bodice. A black garter belt circled her waist. Below it her white buttocks gleamed in the light as I pushed the dress to her stockinged thighs, then to the floor.

Naked except for black garter belt and black nylons, she walked across the room to the writing desk. She picked up the check and held it out to me.

"Take it, David. Put it in your wallet."

She waited until the wallet was back in my pocket. Then she said, "Take off your clothes now." She watched, standing there with her breasts hard and solid, brown nipples jutting stiffly. Her eyes widened as my boxer shorts went down.

"Your Babette got you all excited, didn't she?"

I think I could have killed her right then.

"You want to make love to me, don't you, David?"

"Yes. I want to make love to you."

Why deny it? She smiled faintly and put a cigarette between her lips and clicked the lighter. She shook her head. "I think I've been excessively cruel to you lately. I think I tend to forget you're so young—so healthy." She blew smoke at me. "There are ways to keep you in line besides money—so that you will ignore any more Babettes you meet."

She continued to smoke, knowing I could not look away from her. She did some looking herself and she enjoyed what she was seeing. There was the cruelty of the cat in this woman. She must mock and tease and taunt to show her authority.

"Kneel down, David," she said lazily.

I knelt. She told me to beg.

So I begged, kneeling there in front of her.

The night became an endless cascade of fleshly pleasures. For once, Felicia was not the cool, self-possessed woman of the world but a screaming, writhing female hunting satiation, clawing at my flesh, goading me with whispered obscenities. We did not love so much as wage a kind of war, there in her bed. There was a desperate need in her to subdue me, to hear me acknowledge that she was the winner in this sensual, delirious battle.

I grew aware that a part of me was retreating before this queer aberration that clutched her. A part of me wanted out, wanted freedom from this woman, but another part was wallowing in the dregs of passion her flesh was offering. I fought with her for the victory—for a victory which, in my heart, I understood I could never have.

"If this is what you want, this is what you get," she panted sometime during the night. "Is this what you want, David?" she asked as her fingers fondled me.

"Yes. Yes, yes!"

The ship throbbed on under us, cleaving its passage through the water. Its motors hummed like the beating of a mighty heart. We were one with the ship, bathed in its electric lights, tumbled together on one of its beds. I felt as if I were the ship itself, powerful, unstoppable, surging forward to a preordained port. Or else I was the wind whipping across the waves, elemental, fierce, without heart, without conscience—uncaring.

There was no night and no dawn under the brilliant bedroom lamps. There was only this white witch with her swollen breasts, trembling buttocks, writhing hips, and the things we did to one another. Our hoarse cries, our gaspings, made a symphony of lust in the cabin air. When at last I rolled free I felt like dying. I was exhausted.

Her hand touched me. She moved over me.

"No," I whispered. "No more."

"I thought you wanted loving, David. Come on!"

I pushed her away. She laughed mockingly.

Her face came between me and the ceiling as she looked down at me. There were dark rings under her purple eyes and her hair was wet with sweat and matted to her skull, but she was laughing. I saw her even white teeth and her red tongue in a mouth open in derision.

"I won, I won," she chanted down into my upturned face. "I exhausted you. I wore you out, lover."

I nodded. "You won," I acknowledged hoarsely.

I fell asleep with Felicia Marr grinning down at me.

I never saw Babette Famieux again. Either she transferred herself to the tourist cabins or Felicia Marr had her transferred. Knowing Felicia, the move probably cost her a big sum of money. Or maybe not; maybe Babette was too mad not to go by herself, without being paid. I never knew. I did not ask and Felicia volunteered no information.

There was a change in Felicia after that night.

It was as if I had lighted a fire in her flesh. She would swim in the pool and bake in the sun during the mornings, but in the afternoons I had to stay in the cabin and make love to her. She could not get enough of my body. Perhaps she was trying to prove something to herself as well as to me, that it was not only the young who could love endlessly and continually.

I spent more time in her stateroom than in my own— the long afternoons and then the endless nights, after dinner and a couple of cocktails. We never played bridge any more. We shunned the ship's theater. It was just Felicia and me in her cabin, on her bed, with the god of love chuckling at our antics.

Antics? There is no other word to describe what we did in her stateroom. We sampled the love positions of a world, the varying caresses by which a man and a woman can show their desire for one another. I taught her things of which she had not dreamed; she in turn became my teacher. We were not lovers so much as we were madman and madwoman. She was driven by her compulsion, I by some inner need to justify my existence in my own eyes. In a sort of insane reasoning I told myself that she paid me to make love to her and if it killed me I was going to see that she got her money's worth.

By the time we docked at La Havre, we both needed a vacation.

Felicia told me she had changed our plans.

"On account of you, you naughty boy," she said lazily, standing beside me at the rail and watching the shore loom large before us. "Instead of staying in Paris we'll go on to Rome. Or, at least, I'll go to Rome."

"Oh? Where will I go?"

"To Capri. You're going to find us a place to stay for a

couple of weeks, a place where we can sop up sunshine and just loaf. No sight-seeing. Not for a while. Then maybe we can make your tour."

I never argued with Felicia any more. She had too many ways to strike back at me. I only nodded and told her I liked her change in plan.

"Two weeks in Capri sounds like paradise," I commented.

She patted my hand. "It will be."

And it was. Only not the way Felicia Marr thought.

We flew to Rome by Air France.

In Rome I saw her settled in a suite of rooms at the Grand Hotel. She pushed a thousand dollars in fives and tens into my hands, telling me I could change it into lire, wherever and whenever I wanted. Right now she had to sleep. She had an important date with her agents for the following day.

I rented a car, a little Bugatti that had seen better days but was still in good working order. I drove southward by way of what, in ancient times, had been the Via Latina, by-passing Frascati and heading straight toward Naples. It was a drive of two hundred kilometers but I drove as if the devil himself—or his number one handmaiden—were on my taillights, taking the narrow bends on two wheels in a cloud of dust and pressing my accelerator to the floorboards on the straightaways. For the first time in months (it seemed like eternity) I was off by myself, with money in my wallet and a good car under my rump.

And with no Felicia Marr to bug me.

I sang as I eased the car down the hilly roads and along the floor of the valley of the Liris—in English, in French, in Italian. I even tried Latin once, but I got to laughing so much I damn near took off the near rear wheel of a cart as I swept past it to the accompaniment of its driver's screamed curses. I went back to Italian.

Man, I felt good.

When it started to get dark I pulled into the yard of a roadside inn, nosed the Bugatti into a stable and locked it. The roadside inn was clean, its food was good, its wines fair. I ate and drank like a glutton, then fell into bed before eleven o'clock.

Next morning I met Renata.

She was pushing a little two-wheeled cart ahead of her, up a narrow road. The cart was filled with fish. I neither

117

knew her name nor the fact that there were fish under the striped, faded tarpaulin when I came around the bend.

She heard me coming and moved to one side to let me pass. Unfortunately, her sandaled foot slid on a pebble. The weight of the cart pulled its worn wooden handles from her fingers and it started downhill to meet me.

I braked the Bugatti and skidded.

The cart banged into me and turned over. Fish went flying through the air as if some perverse god had flung them. I damn near drowned in fish before I got the car stopped, up against a hedge. There must have been fifty mullet, carp and sole in the open seat beside me. I know damn well there was a grayling half inside my shirt.

"Eeeaggh," said a voice.

It was like a scream and a laugh rolled into one, shouted by an angel with a silver tongue. I wanted to be mad. I wanted to be hopping mad—mad enough to sock somebody. All I did was sit there foolishly, watching a girl laugh her head off at me.

Her mirth was so infectious, I chuckled. Then I started laughing just as hard. She came over to the car and gripped its door with both hands, looking in at me and the fish and screaming until the tears ran down her tanned cheeks. She was an earthy Cytherea.

Judging by her plain red-wool skirt and faded blouse, she was no rich man's daughter. Her brown hair had come undone with her laughter so that it lay tumbled around her tanned shoulders where the low peasant blouse bared them. Her mouth was a ripe red fruit, her eyes long-lashed and slumberous. With the heels of her dirty palms she wiped the tear streaks from her cheeks. It pleased me that she could laugh to see all these fish wasted like that.

She clapped a hand to her mouth and stared over her fingers at me when I mentioned this. Her eyes became enormous with tragedy. "Mamma *mia*," she whimpered. "She will kill me! *Santa Maria benedetta!* I am lost."

"It isn't as bad as all that," I told her, throwing fish out into the dusty road. The Bugatti would stink for weeks.

"Ma si, ma si, ma si," she kept moaning, slapping her hand on the side of the overturned cart. "You do not know my mother. She is one wild woman when she gets mad. *Dio mio!* Don't I know? My behind—"

She flushed and looked away. I grinned. "Tanned you good, hey? For being naughty with the fishing boys, no doubt."

118

Her hip swung insultingly but she glanced sideways from under long brown lashes. She studied my grin awhile, then laughed, shaking her head.

"I do not know why I laugh. I am mad—just like you. These fish are all that will keep us in food and clothes for the next few days, until I have the boat fixed. Now—now look at them!" Her dirty hand bade me study the scattered carcasses of the sole and carp. She was tragedy in dirty feet. She clapped her hands to her face and her shoulders heaved as she wailed.

"Oh, hell," I said. "I'll pay for the goddamn fish."

Her fingers opened and her dark eyes peeped between them at me. "How much?" she wanted to know.

"A dollar," I said brutally, just to watch her reaction.

She opened her mouth and bawled louder.

"Two," I muttered hastily.

She kept right on screeching.

"Ten—if you give me a kiss," I suggested.

Her hands came down and she looked at the Bugatti, at my clothes and finally at my face. She made a rude noise and turned her back, but she did not move away. Her hips worked back and forth, indignation in red wool. I tossed the last fish over my shoulder and stepped up behind her.

"My dear young lady—"

"I'm not your dear young lady. I'm not your anything."

"All right, not-my-anything, I'll—"

She laughed, mirth bubbling inside her with a spontaneity that held me spellbound. She turned and with both fists planted on her hips she told me things that held me speechless—about my ancestry and my family, about my nose and ears and eyes.

"Fifty," I said suddenly

I caught her between words. She drew a deep breath. "Fifty?"

"Fifty American dollars."

"For what?" she asked darkly with suspicion. I spread my hands innocently. "For the fish, of course. What else?"

"For a kiss," she muttered sullenly.

I gestured airily. "I never pay for kisses. I take them."

She was drawing a breath to tell me what she thought about the rest of me, I suppose—she was a great talker—when I put my arms about her slim middle and kissed her. She lay against me soft and warm for only a moment, but in that second I could feel her hips and breasts like fire on me.

119

She struggled, I give her that; but what had begun as a joke, I continued because it was so good. I do not say I fell in love with Renata Delabba at that instant, but if there is such a thing as love at first sight, I had it. She reached inside me with her eyes and her lips and her body and held me tightly.

Her fists banged my shoulders, my back. Later it dawned on me that she could just as easily have hit my face, or clawed it, but not right then. I thought she was battling with all her strength. I let her go after a while and watched her rub her lips with the back of her hand. Her breasts bounced wildly under her worn blouse. One thing for sure I knew by this time: she didn't wear a brassiere.

"Pig! Big boar! Son of a—"

She broke off at sight of my wallet. I counted out two twenties and a ten-spot. As she reached for them I held them away. "I'll need a boat to get me to Capri," I told her. "I'm going to stay there for a couple of weeks."

"All alone?"

"All alone—except for a possible visitor. But for a few days at least, all alone."

"A boat you need. Our boat is broken."

"Fifty dollars will fix it soon enough."

"Oh, *si*. I guess so."

"Tomorrow morning at the Pozzuoli wharf."

"You know Pozzuoli?"

I shrugged. "Enough to get by. I've been here before."

"All right. A boat for Capri in the morning."

"With you in it."

She looked at me from under those long lashes as if to say that like all Americans I was stupid as well as rich. Did I think she was going to let me slip out of her clutches and into the hands of some hussy who preyed on helpless boys like me, with too much money and not enough brains? Certainly not!

She took the money and put it into the blouse.

ELEVEN

I was waiting on the quay at Pozzuoli next morning when the boat hove into view. It was an old tub, its paint peeling, its motors chugging steadily in a coughing gurgle. Almost without realizing it, I was holding my breath. It seemed that any second might see the motors wheeze to a stop, or the boat itself slip downward into the waves its blunt prow was slicing with such lazy grace. The girl was standing on the deck; when I saw her I forgot about the boat.

She had bathed and dressed herself in her finery, a black wool jersey that clung to her body as though it were elastic, a colorful sash of reds and blues and yellows wrapped about her middle, and a skirt of gray flannel. She waved and laughed, her hair blowing free about her shoulders.

"Buon giorno, Americano."

"Buon giorno to you, little one," I called back. "Is the boat safe for one more passenger?"

"She will live longer than you and I put together. Are you ready to go to Capri?"

I had my single valise on the planks beside me; the Bugatti was housed by the week in a garage; Felicia Marr was safe in Rome with her business agents; I was ripe for a holiday. A sea wind had come into the harbor with the boat, and now it blew in my face as though in welcome. I laughed at its touch, watching the girl run back to the wheel she had momentarily abandoned to come and wave at me.

The old tire hanging on the portside bow bumped a piling. The boat nosed around. I leaped from the quay and landed on its deck, waving an arm at the girl and shouting. *"Fa subito, fa subito."*

She laughed, showing white teeth. "Nobody ever hurries here. What are you running from—the *carabinieri?"*

"Nothing as bad as that," I told her, and crossed mental fingers against the thought of Felicia Marr. "I just want to get away from everything back there, to start life over again."

"You crazy American! A man can never run away from himself."

I sat on a worn bench near the taffrail so that I was within reach of the girl as her strong, tanned hands swung the wheel. Her breasts jounced in the black wool to the movements of her arms, and where the wool stretched a little more than usual, I thought I could make out flesh tints.

"I don't even know your name. Mine's David Horne."

"David is a nice name. Mine's Renata. Renata Delabba."

"A heavenly name—to go with the scenery."

The green waters, and the sunlight glimmering on the

121

houses of Pozzuoli, on the washing that hung from their upper windows, on an occasional iron balcony fronting a shuttered door or window, added up to something from a master's canvas. The bricks and claywork of the town seemed dipped in gold where the sun touched them. In the distance, Capri was a blue hump rising from the waters.

"I suppose there are a lot of tourists on the island?"

"There are always tourists."

"I wanted to get away from crowds," I told her. Then I asked, "Where do you live?"

"In a little cottage a few miles from Pozzuoli."

"Do you take in boarders?"

She looked over her shoulder at me, her eyes calculating. It was as if she had an adding machine in her head. I grinned at her, saying, "I can pay my way. Say . . . ten American dollars a week? Twenty?"

"Do you eat much?" she wondered cautiously.

"Only what you'll feed me."

"Thirty dollars," she announced firmly.

It would be a fortune to her family, and it made me feel good to know it. I was damn tired of being given money; for a change I wanted to do the giving, to help someone. I told her it was a deal and she looked pleased. She wanted to know if she should turn back.

"No, go around the island. I haven't been here in a couple of years. I want to see if it's changed very much."

Capri was still the same—an island with rock sides, seventeen miles out in the Mediterranean from Naples. It is an old island to mankind. The emperor Tiberius Caesar sported here in the grottoes that line its coast, and before him the Etruscans, and perhaps before them the Phoenicians. The sun is warm, the air cool and filled with a winy tang that makes a mockery of trouble and anxiety.

As we neared its green slopes and the villas that dotted them like toy castles, I thought back to the old legend which calls Capri the island of Sirens, where Ulysses tied himself to his mast to avoid their call. It was an unofficial playground of the International Set. You could bump into a *contessa* or a princess or a movie star walking across a wide piazza, or you could drink espresso coffee or wine in a fisherman's bar at four in the morning. You wore what clothes you wanted and, so long as you did not infringe on the rights of others, you could do just about whatever struck your fancy. It was a vision dreamed up by a jaded sophisticate.

And yet it did not appeal to me.

For a little while, as I stared at the island and its grottoes, I told himself I was sick. Somewhere I'd picked up a bug that had affected my mind. I'd been anxious to get to Capri, anxious to take a *sandalino* into its Blue Grotto, eager to swim in the crystal waters off the Marina Piccola. Now none of it mattered to me.

Without seeming to do so, I looked at Renata.

There was a freshness about her, an air of unspoiled honesty that touched me deep inside. Maybe it was because all my life I'd been on the receiving end, first from my adoptive father, then from the rich women off whose generosity and carnal appetites I had made my living. I had never been asked to give, either of money or of myself. For the first time, I had found a human being who looked up to me, who turned to me for help, instead of me to her.

It was a new feeling for David Mason Horne—a warm feeling, an emotion that made my chest swell proudly, that made my head stand higher on my shoulders. I felt like yelling, jumping.

"You know," I said suddenly. "I think I could fix your motor for you. It sounds like an old car I once had. Maybe five, six dollars worth of parts and you won't know the old tub."

"Who will pay for the parts?"

"I will, since it's my idea. We could call it part of my board."

"All right. When will you fix it?"

"Tomorrow morning."

Right now I wanted to savor this new sensation and so I walked away from Renata and paced along the port rail, watching Capri enlarge before me. A group of swimmers in a *sandalino* waved. I waved back, thinking they were a part of my world, the real world, that this boat and the girl on it were a dream from which I would eventually awake.

The island is only four square miles of earth and rock. We were soon around it and chugging back toward Positano where Renata had her home.

"Can you steer a boat?" she wondered suddenly.

When I told her I could, she looked dubious but determined. This was too good a chance to pass up, she informed me, so if I was willing she would put down the fishing nets while she was out here. The boat would be going slowly so there would be no danger, she assured me. I wondered what danger there might be in these waters; then I remembered she thought me a stupid American.

She went into the little cabin and took off her good clothes, emerging in a patched skirt and a reasonably clean white blouse. Her working clothes, she told me, and she went to work with a will. Her young body was strong, lithe. The nets seemed weightless the way she handled them. Soon they were overside and we crawled through the Tyrrhenian sunshine, dragging them behind us.

I took off my coat, my shirt, sat naked to my middle in the sun, letting it warm me. There was approval in her eyes as they studied my chest and arms. After a while she came and sat beside me.

The sun shone down, the boat slipped along lazily through the water, and Renata was beside me. It was corny, but it was good. I think, for the first time in a long time, I was actually happy. I put my arm about her shoulders, drew her toward me.

Instantly she was suspicious. At the same time she seemed to sense my gesture had been made in good fellowhip, not in desire. She laughed and put her head on my shoulder.

"You are a funny one, David."

"How so?"

"You are like a little boy on a holiday."

"Not your idea of a rich American playboy?"

She shook her head. "No. But I like you."

As if she were afraid of what she had said, she left the curve of my arm and went walking up and down the deck, turning to glance back at me every so often. I had an idea about Renata Delabba then. Maybe—just maybe—she was falling in love with me and was frightened by what was happening to her. I told myself I was nuts. A girl as pretty as she must have a lot of boy friends. Then I remembered that in Italy, among the poorer people, a girl was looked after pretty strictly.

It was just possible.

We spent the afternoon drawing the nets in our wake, eating lunch together—she had prepared salami sandwiches and a jug of wine she cooled by dropping it overside with a towrope attached to it—and baking in the sun. When the sun got too hot I went into the cabin and put on my swim trunks.

I dove overside and swam around while she went on with the boat, making a great arc and coming back for me when I'd had enough of the water. I felt refreshed, vigorous. I stood on the deck dripping water on it and sang.

She howled with laughter at my voice. She sang the same song the way it should be sung. She had a good voice —not a great one—and she could have made money on the night-club circuit back home, especially with her looks. I found myself scowling, not liking the idea. It would be like taking a fish out of water. She had not been made for night clubs.

When the sun touched the western horizon, she turned the boat around and headed for home. Our first day together was coming to an end. I felt a strange sadness.

The Delabbas lived in a white stucco farmhouse bordered by a stone wall, by wide green fields and meadows, by a big stable the roof of which was badly in need of repair, and a number of chicken houses fenced about with wire. It looked dilapidated, but with an air of decay that speaks of better days, like an old roué on his last legs. Once it had been a prosperous farm, it seemed to say; once it had gleamed with paint and polish. The fact that the days of its glory might have been two centuries ago did not matter; there was a timelessness about it that drew you into its aura.

A boy was standing in the yard staring as we came through the gate. There was a shyness in him that made him move back toward the shelter of the front doorway. Renata called to him with a laugh, naming him Francesco, telling him to tell Mamma she was back with a guest.

There was no need to tell Mamma anything. She was opening the door and standing there, wiping her hands on an apron, a surprisingly pretty woman, plump and with a happy, open face. I could see where Renata got her looks. Gianetta Delabba made me welcome to her home, glancing first at Renata, then at me. Whatever she saw in our faces seemed somehow to please her.

There was no father, but there were a few photos of him on the fireplace mantel and in a big leather album, and a lonesome grave back under the olive trees on the hillside. Roberto Delabba had died nine years ago, right after young Francesco had been born. It had been a struggle for Gianetta Delabba after that, trying to make the farm— and the boat that was to have been the start of a fishing fleet for Delabba e Figlio—pay off. Renata had been almost ten at the time.

125

I did not learn this all at once. At first the family was shy with me, all except Renata, who regarded me as her own property. It came in dribs and drabs over the days, at breakfast and at dinner, in the cool morning hours when I was painting the woodwork of the house or hammering nails into the beams that would take a new stable roof.

For I worked every day. I worked as I had not worked in years, because I wanted to—as once I had worked at the Horne estate in Loudoun County during Christmas vacations and at midterm breaks. I had learned to handle a hammer and a saw in those days, together with a paint-brush, from a big blond man named Svensen, who was the overseer of the estate. Now I was glad I had.

Renata protested a little, her mother a lot, as I busied myself at this task and that around the place. "You are on a vacation. This sort of thing is not for you."

"You want me to have a good time, don't you?" I would ask. "I enjoy doing it. I'm having fun. As everyone seems to think, I am a stupid American."

It was the one argument that always worked. Gianetta would tap her forehead with a fingertip and walk away, shrugging me off as no worry of hers. If I wanted to spend my money on paint and nails and timber, it was a reflection of my own particular madness.

I was not always working. I went out with Renata when she thought the fish were running. Our first afternoon resulted in a fine catch of carp and mullet, several thousand *lire* worth of good eating to be sold to the Neapolitan hotels and restaurants, which went in heavily for sea food on their menus. I think Renata regarded me much as she might a good-luck charm, after that haul.

Our days on the boat were the happiest of all, I think. We were alone with the wide ocean and the boat for our world, and it was all we asked. We had slipped into a gay camaraderie together, laughing and joking, and sometimes we kissed when the hot Italian sun bubbled our blood enough.

Later I understood it was a waiting time for both of us.

Renata wanted to see me in many moods before she would listen to the pulse of her young blood, her hungry body. We joked about it, but there was a grain of suspicion behind her opinion that I was a crazy Americano. I didn't help matters any by turning myself into a general handyman around the boat and the farm, either. What kind of vacation was it where the vacationer worked his fingers to the bone with chores around the hillside farm, or on an old tub of a boat, with fishing nets and motors? That was the part of it they could not understand.

Sometimes I wondered if Felicia Marr was looking for me, but as I hammered away at a roofing nail, putting the last few shingles in place on the big stable, I knew I did not care. The hell with Felicia Marr. I whistled and went on hammering.

It was the same way with the nets. I think I worried just as much, if not more, than Renata when they came up empty or with so few fish they would hardly make a good meal for the little Delabba family and its guest. I know damn well I scanned the waters just as eagerly as she, to try and spot the signs betraying the fact that sole or grayling were somewhere in the vicinity.

One day I went and got the Bugatti and brought it back to the farm so I could take Renata, her mother and her brother, dressed all in their best clothes, somewhat worn but clean and passable, to dinner at a Neapolitan restaurant. Another day we drove to the beach at Positano—it was too filled with pebbles for my liking but the Delabbas considered it a paradise—where I pretended to ogle the girls in their bikinis while Renata glowered at me, telling me I should be ashamed of myself. Her mother, with a faint sigh but with a twinkle in her eyes, explained that all men were basically the same, easily attracted by a shapely leg or a pair of large breasts.

There was a night when Renata and I went to the ballet to see Lucienne Pedrini. Afterwards we drove through the cool night with her head on my shoulder and her hand clasping mine. Never in my entire life had I felt so close to anyone as I felt to Renata Delabba that evening. It was a blend of her presence and her open enjoyment of the ballet, the music, even the after-the-show ices we ate at a sidewalk café.

It was that night, I think, that set me to planning an escape from Felicia Marr. True, she had no such hold over me as she had over Dori Pierce or Doctor Vance, but I knew her well enough to understand that she considered me her private property, her own little plaything. She would fight like hell to keep me from getting away.

And Felicia Marr fought real dirty.

I bought a bikini for Renata one afternoon in Naples, a black strip of silk for her loins, another for her breasts. All I needed was the courage to give it to her. She was not the

127

sort of girl who paraded around in front of the world—as do the girls on the beaches at the Riviera, at St. Tropitz, Capri and other holiday spots on the continent—for everyone to know what she looked like naked.

So I made a joke of it.

I produced the bikini one night after we had dined to fatness on veal cacciatore, saying that next time we went to the Positano beach she could wear it. Gianetta gasped and looked at her daughter. Renata colored slightly, glancing at me from under her long brown lashes, then picked up the two narrow strips and held them to her body.

"Would you want me to wear this at Positano?"

It was my turn to be embarrassed. I growled something and reached for the things. She whisked them out of the way behind her back. She began to laugh softly to herself. To my surprise her mother was humming, and knitting, the picture of composure. Apparently she had discovered something. About Renata? About me? That made her very happy.

"I will keep it," Renata told me, wriggling away when I reached to tear the bikini from her hands by sheer force. "There is a mirror in my room. I will put it on and see how I look in it."

She moved off, her buttocks twitching gently.

I did not see Renata in the bikini for a few days; I was too busy around the farm and tinkering with the motor of the fishing tub. Every day I spent an hour, before darkness, taking the motor apart, putting it back together again after cleaning and sandpapering some of the dirtier parts. I put in new spark plugs, new pistons, valve heads, points. I fussed with that old engine as if it had been the latest thing off a Ferrari assembly line. I polished every moving part and replaced the propeller. I all but rebuilt the damn thing.

While I worked on the motor, Renata and her mother labored with spanking new paint brushes in their hands. I told them they could make more money with the boat as a tourist attraction than they could as a fishing smack. Renata knew the coast and its waters. She could even give a little lecture on Capri, on Naples and its magnificent bay.

"Charge five dollars for the trip. Anybody worth taking on the boat can afford a measly five bucks. Feed them, if it will make you feel better—something exotic they can't usually get in a restaurant."

They were like children with this idea, but they realized

they had to have a fine, clean boat and so they worked as hard as I did. At the end of ten days the boat was ready for its first trip. It shone from prow to stern with fresh red and white paint and with new brass fittings I'd ordered.

"First trip for the workers," announced Renata.

Her mother had prepared a lunch. We set out early in the morning and went around Capri, Renata practicing her little speech, then straightened out to run for Amalfi. We put on bathing suits in the privacy of the cabin and went swimming before we turned back.

By five in the afternoon we were dropping anchor beside the farmhouse. While her mother and young Francesco went to prepare supper, Renata and I decided to take the boat out to Capri, then dive overboard for a swim near the Blue Grotto. While I handled the wheel, Renata went into the cabin. She was gone for about five minutes.

When she came out, she was wearing the bikini.

I stared at her. It was hard to breathe, seeing her young body encased in those two narrow black bands. Her tanned legs were long, slim, firmly fleshed, and the cloth at her loins hid very little. Her belly was a gentle mound with deepset navel. Above it, her large breasts rode gently to her every step.

She flushed as my eyes went over her, but she stood proudly, aware that she was lovely. I think she wanted this to be a special moment between us, because she came right up to me and stood there waiting.

"I love you," I told her simply.

She looked toward the island off our port bow.

"I want to marry you," I added.

Her large, dark eyes turned to stare at me. "You are sure?" she asked breathlessly. "You do not say this just to— to get me to let you make love to me?"

"I'll go into Naples in the morning, find a priest, bring him out to the farm."

She put her arms around me and pressed into me, kissing me with open lips, hungrily. There was a warmth to her skin that made me tremble. I understood that Renata was playing for keeps, that she wanted me as her own, for all time, or not at all.

I wanted it the same way between us. I was tired of Felicia Marr and her world, the sophistication of casual affairs and intermittent beddings. I had enough money put away for Renata and me to get a good start. I could make the farm and the boat pay handsome dividends. A little

129

American know-how would make the farm fields fertile and rich. Until this happened, the boat and guided tours would keep us in clothes and food.

We dove overboard, side by side. We swam together, innocent as children, not touching one another because we had agreed to wait until after the priest had wedded us. At least, this was our intention; the reality was something else again. She was as good as naked in the black bikini. I wore only the narrow trunks which most men wore at the Riviera and Positano beaches. We were both young, both healthy. The cool bay waters were invigorating.

It happened when we bumped at the foot of the ladder before ascending to the deck. We were still in the water, our hands on the ladder rungs. Our bodies touched. I felt her buttocks press into my loins; she felt the instant response of my body to that accidental touching. She half turned. Her eyes were wide, fearful, yet filled with passion; they seemed to glow as if a fire had been lighted deep in their depths. My hand went down her bare wet back to stroke her flesh where the bikini bottoms failed to cover her.

Renata put a slick wet arm about my neck. Her eyes were half closed. "Take away your hand," she breathed. "It excites me too much."

"I'm excited, too," I said simply.

"Do you want me so badly?"

"Very badly. Can't you tell?"

Her mouth bored into mine. She used the hand that held the ladder rung to urge herself closer through the water, to let me understand the hardness of her breasts that were big and swollen, almost pushing their way out of the thin black band that held them. She moved her breasts back and forth, panting softly into my mouth.

My hands went to her bikini trunks, slid them off her hips. She gasped when my hands stroked her flesh, when I pushed her so that her shoulders wedged into the ladder. I slipped my hands under her armpits so she could rest them on my wrists as I held the rungs. Then I doubled my legs up so I could slide my own suit down.

We were protected from the island by the bulk of the ship. At my back was the vast, empty expanse of Mediterranean. For an instant I wondered how many others had made love this way, in these waters, but then she was drawing me to her, breathing harshly, her eyes closed and her head fallen back a little so that her loosened black hair fell over my hands and the ladder rungs.

She gasped, moaning deep in her throat; then it was all right for her, and she moved with me, slowly and with rapture. I looked down into her face, the eyes closed, the full red lips parted slightly so I caught a glimpse of white teeth. Drops of water shook loose from her face and, as she moved more fully, her body made little wavelets around us.

The water cradled us for an eternity of pleasure.

Twice she opened her eyes to stare up at me in awed acknowledgment of these sensual spasms which held her in their grip. Her arms were velvet bands that held me prisoner to her tireless body.

It lasted a long time.

Until we were both changed, somehow, deep inside us. I'd told this girl I loved her, that I wanted to marry her; I had only spoken words. Now I knew the real meaning of what I'd said. If I had to live away from her, I'd die or go nuts. It was that simple. She had become my life. And she felt the same way. Inside me, I knew it.

When it was over, she leaned forward and put her head on my chest. There was no sorrow in her for her lost virginity; she accepted the fact as a part of life. She was my woman now. Everything she had belonged to me.

"I'll go get the priest as soon as we dock," I told her. She only nodded against my chest so that her hair made a tickling sensation on my flesh.

When she shivered, I said, "We'd better get out of the water." My hand was on her back but I felt no brassiere cord. She'd lost the top part of the bikini, too. She laughed when I told her.

"When we are married, you will buy me a new bikini. You will show me off when we go to Positano. The young men will look at me and they will envy you very much."

"They sure will, honey."

She pinched me and turned to mount the ladder.

Her mother only nodded when I told her at the dinner table that I was going into Naples to see a priest. Women seem to understand these things far better than men; all it needs is a word or a certain glance, and everything is clear to them. Her mother saw us coming up the path, hand in hand, and something about the way we walked and looked at one another made her realize what had happened between us. She seemed very pleased; at least, she sang while she set the table.

I took the Bugatti, after kissing Renata and promising to be back within the hour. I had no idea what you had to do

131

to get married in Italy, though it did seem that banns had to be published and maybe you even took a blood test; the priest would know all this; whatever he told me, I would do.

I turned at the bend in the hill road to wave back at her. She was standing by the white-fence gate, a scarf in her hand, waving overhead. There was a lump in my throat and a fireball in my middle. She was everything I'd ever wanted in life.

I came into Naples by way of the Strada Belvedere. There was a church Renata had told me about—the Church of Santa Lucia—and a priest named Father Malatesta. I parked the car close by the rectory and moved along the sidewalk toward the high bronze gate that opened onto a little garden path.

It was dark by this time, but not so dark I could not see the three men moving from the shadows beyond the garden wall. There was a big black limousine parked a hundred yards behind the Bugatti. I was aware of all this only remotely; I was too concerned about seeing Father Malatesta to pay attention to anything else. I had never seen the three men before. They had nothing to do with me.

One of them brushed me with a shoulder.

His hand came out and shoved me back. He said something in an Italian dialect I could not understand. The other two men moved closer.

For the first time I knew I was in danger. They were lithe, muscular men—sailors or dockside workers. Any one of them could have taken me in a rough and tumble. And there were three of them.

"Look, there's some mistake," I said placatingly.

"You bumped me, dirty American."

"I'm sorry. I—"

His hand lashed out like the head of a darting snake. It took me on the chin, rocked my head back. Before I could recover, the other two moved in, their fists driving for my face. Knuckles landed sideways on my nose and I heard the crunch of cartilage. Another fist caught me on the side of my jaw. Then the first one was hammering at my belly.

It was as if various parts of me had exploded suddenly with pain. I went back two steps, sick with the agony in my middle where the man had hit me three inches below my belt buckle. My own fist drove out, landed hard. I heard a man grunt.

Then they were all over me, the three of them, cutting me off from everything but the world of their fists, their uplifting knees, their kicking feet. The dull impact of heavy blows was in my ears, together with a wet gurgling sound that I realized, after a while, was my own breath sobbing in my throat. I tried to fight back, but it was useless.

I fell hard to my knees. It was a mistake. A foot slammed into my face. I went backwards only to meet a second boot between my shoulder blades. It drove me forward so that a heel could take me at the base of my neck.

My face went into the pavement.

Hands lifted me to my feet and the fists and knees and shoes began all over again. Once I think I screamed when a foot rammed my groin. I began to retch, staggering on widespread legs, eyes swollen and half blind. My nose had been broken. My ribs felt as if they were on fire. I wanted to die.

I fell down. I was picked up.

The fists slammed me. The knees thudded hard against me. The kicking went on and on. I was a big straw doll without any life by this time. My muscles could not hold me erect. Two of the men had to support me by the arms while a third worked over what was left of my face.

Then they stopped. I hung limp.

I smelled perfume. Vaguely I was aware that I had been smelling that sweet musky scent all during the fight. I tried to open my eyes. They were swollen too tightly. But there was nothing wrong with my ears.

"Thank you, gentlemen," said Felicia Marr.

"It was a pleasure, madame."

"You've earned your fifty thousand *lire* apiece. Now for another fifty thousand, help him to my car."

The hands lifted, carrying me so my feet scraped the sidewalk. I was in a red world of pain where only sound and my own maddened thoughts existed. I thought of Renata and the priest, and of our marriage that would never be. Maybe Felicia Marr would have me killed and my body dumped somewhere. I wanted to cry. I couldn't even do that.

My body flopped bonelessly into the tonneau of the big limousine. Felicia got in beside me. She sat at a little distance from me, probably not wanting to get her dress dirty with my blood. The motor hummed to life. The car moved.

After a little while, Felicia spoke again. "David? Can

133

you hear me? Where does your little whore live—this girl with whom you have been carrying on?"

I wanted to open my mouth, to move my tongue and tell her to go to hell. All I could do was moan. Apparently it satisfied her.

"I would send those men to do the same thing to her, if I knew. Perhaps they would do more than beat her up. You would not like that, would you, David?"

Now I could cry, thinking about that. And I did, the tears rolling in great drops down my bleeding, bruised cheeks. I was crying for Renata and me and our lost happiness. In a sense, I was crying a requiem for Felicia Marr, too.

She was going to die.

To keep her away from Renata, I would kill her.

TWELVE

FOR A WEEK and a half I lay in a hotel bed, attended by a day and a night nurse. A doctor came to visit me twice a day. The story got out that I had been attacked by a band of vicious youths, that Felicia Marr had found me lying unconscious in a Neapolitan gutter and had brought me to her hotel to be attended to. She was the great lady, *la gran signora,* to the hotel staff, to the nurses and the doctor.

Only to me was she herself.

She would come into my room at night, after sending the nurse out for a breath of air. She would seat herself on the edge of the bed and wonder out loud about how I would look when the bandages were cut away.

"You will no longer be so handsome, David dear. Little harlots like your Renata Delabba—oh, yes! I've found out who she is and where she lives—will no longer be so enamored of you. Did I ever tell you that money can buy anything? Isn't that how I found you, with money?"

She had hired every private detective in the city to track me down. Her agents had gone around with hundreds of photographs, passing them out to trades people, to postmen, to peddlers, to police officers.

The headwaiter in the Neapolitan restaurant where the Delabbas and I had eaten remembered me. So did an usher at the ballet. A farmer from beyond Pozzuoli had noticed me in the Bugatti. Her men began to search for it.

The night I had been beaten up, a phone call was bringing her to Pozzuoli when she passed me in the Bugatti on my way to see Father Malatesta. Felicia had ordered the limousine turned around to follow me. They had kept me in view until I parked. Then the three hoodlums had climbed out of the car and approached.

She no longer threatened Renata, I noticed.

"The poor darling really isn't to blame, is she, David? It was all your fault, wasn't it?"

"All my fault," I mumbled through the bandages.

"Of course, if you should start acting up, I can always send those hoodlums to find her. Your dear Renata will be a sword of Damocles hanging over your head, to compel your obedience."

My body was young. It healed quickly. Inside of three days the bandages were off. One of the nurses held a mirror in front of me and I saw my face for the first time since I had been beaten up. My nose was broken. The doctor had done his best to reset it, but it was awry. My eyes were darkly ringed and swollen. A couple of my teeth were gone. I was a mess.

My broken ribs took longer to heal. At the end of the week I was hobbling around the hotel room in my pajamas. I could sit in a chair now while Felicia talked to me.

"I'm sending you home, away from temptation, David. I'll fly to London, once you're on your way, and get my business done there as quickly as possible. I want to keep my eye on you, to prevent you from getting into trouble. You'll do just what I say from now on, David. Because if you don't, you know what will happen to Renata."

That was the hell of it. I knew only too well. I told myself there was only one way for me ever to regain my liberty from Felicia Marr.

She had to die.

All the way from Naples to London in the big Stratocruiser, I thought about ways and means of killing her. I'd read my share of murder mysteries. I knew how criminals always make a mistake, always left some clue around for detectives to find. I wanted no part of that. I didn't want just to kill Felicia Marr. I wanted to do it in a way that would leave me scot-free.

In London I switched over to the Pan Am President Special. I sipped champagne over the Atlantic and enjoyed the liqueurs and the airborne meal served by Maxim's in Paris, but I still had no idea how I was going to do away with Felicia Marr.

For the three weeks that Felicia Marr stayed on in Europe, I played golf. It was the one way I knew of keeping my sanity. Hitting a ball, driving and putting, I did not remember Renata so vividly. It was only at night, just before falling asleep, that I could not put her out of my mind.

What was she doing? Did she ever wonder what had become of me? She must think me a goddamn rat to run out on her. I'd had her—and then I'd left her. It would be how her mind would work. Hell, it was the way anyone's mind would work.

I debated writing to her but I knew it would do no good. Felicia would have thought of it and would have taken steps to prevent it. I wanted nothing to happen to Renata. She was like a lifesaver to a sinking man. I dared let nothing happen to her. Without her I would have no reason to go on living. I might even kill Felicia Marr just for the pleasure of seeing her die.

Then one day when I came back from the golf course, I saw three automobiles parked in the drive; one of them was her black Cadillac; Felicia had come home. I put my clubs away and went down into the kitchen to find Mrs. Bennett preparing a light snack.

"She looks terrible," Mrs. Bennett told me. "It was that London fog, I'll bet. She's real peaked."

I could muster no sympathy. When she saw it, Mrs. Bennett sniffed. "Thought she was behind whatever happened to you on the other side. Had you beaten up, didn't she? To keep you in line."

"Something like that."

Her hands held out the tray to me. "You want to take this up to her? Doctor Vance is with her."

I shrugged. At least it would give me something to do. Mrs. Bennett had prepared a club sandwich—one of those three-decker things—and some cold milk.

Felicia Marr was in bed, propped up by a couple of pillows. Peaked, Mrs. Bennett had said; she was all of that. Her face was white, drawn, heavily lined. The impish look was gone. She looked her age. Doctor Vance was sitting on the vanity bench, taking her pulse. I came in with the tray.

"David," she said tonelessly.

Doctor Vance pursed his lips. "You're run-down, Felicia.

Your trip was to be a vacation. You made it into something else."

"Did I?" she asked the doctor, but she looked at me.

"You need a good rest."

"I have no time to rest, Thurlow."

"Then a tonic."

"All right, a tonic."

Her purple eyes touched my nose and lips. The nose had healed nicely and a dentist in South Norwalk was working on my teeth. I'd never be the old David Mason Horne, as far as looks went, but whatever money could do to put me back together again, money was doing. Her money, naturally; I was charging everything.

"I'll write out a prescription," Vance muttered.

"No. You make it. David and I will be over later to pick it up." Her voice seemed stronger all of a sudden.

The doctor swiveled around to look at me. His eyes were bland behind his eyeglasses. I wondered what he really thought about me. He nodded slowly, then turned back to his patient.

"All right, Felicia. I'll make it up. You come over to get it any time you want. It'll be ready."

"Maybe you oughtn't to get out of bed," I found myself saying.

Felicia smiled, showing her sharp little teeth. "May I get out of bed, Thurlow?"

He cleared his throat. "Certainly. Nothing wrong with you except you're tired, run-down. Tonic will fix you up, though a week of lazing around Bermuda or the Bahamas would be even better."

"I don't have the time," Felicia said.

"No," said Dori Pierce. "No, you don't."

I turned, not having seen her before. She was in the adjoining bathroom, preparing two tranquilizers and a glass of water. She came toward the bed with them, smiling faintly. "There's the O'Mara job and the Amalgamated lawsuit, and—oh, a hundred things to be looked after."

Felicia took the pills and swallowed them meekly.

Doctor Vance pulled down the blinds and shooed Dori and me out ahead of him, telling us he wanted her to sleep.

Dori and I ate supper together. We said nothing to one another. What had happened between us those weeks ago had been born of liquor and her loneliness. It might hap-

137

pen again—if Felicia let her guard down—but not tonight.

I went to my room and lay on my bed in the darkness, staring blindly upward, hands behind my neck. At eight o'clock or a little after, I would go into Felicia Marr's bedroom and escort her out into the night, to visit Doctor Thurlow Vance. This might be the opportunity I wanted.

An accident along a country road? I could pile up the Starfire against a tree at eighty miles an hour. An instant before it hit I would make a jump for it. I could always say the impact had thrown me clear of the car. Nobody could prove any different.

Felicia would be in the car when it hit. The Starfire had no safety belts. Her head would hit the windshield a good whack. Maybe it would be enough to kill her. If it wasn't I could always crawl to the car and set it on fire. Let her burn to death. Or hit her with a wrench until I broke her skull. Or maybe I could even hold a hand over her mouth, her nose between my thumb and forefinger, just for a little while—until she stopped breathing.

If the sound of the crash didn't bring a lot of witnesses right away, I could always do those things. Maybe if I was real lucky, the crash would be enough.

I lay there and thought about being real lucky.

It was closer to nine than eight when Dori Pierce knocked on my door. "David? Felicia wants to see you."

"Right away," I called.

She was walking around her bedroom in girdle and brassiere. She hadn't put on her stockings yet. She looked better than she had earlier. The sleep and the tranquilizers had done her good. She actually laughed when she saw me and came up against me, lifting her mouth to be kissed. I kissed her. No sense in making her suspicious, I figured.

"Still angry with me, David?"

"Why should I be? You're my bread and butter."

Her eyes flickered at that, but she tried to smile. "I'm glad you see things my way."

"It was the Capri air," I laughed. "It made me forget my duties. I thought I was a free man. I saw a pretty girl and I made a play for her. No more than that."

Her fingertips touched my nose. "I'm sorry I was so rough about it, darling. You made me quite angry. Mmmm —your new nose becomes you, in a way. You're more manly."

Manly enough to commit murder, you bitch!

My arms squeezed her softness and, against my will, I

138

found myself responding to her near nakedness in the bra and girdle. She laughed throatily, pressing into me.

"We'll have a party soon as we get back," she said, and dragged me down to her hungry lips. Her tongue was thick and wet. After a while she pushed me away and said, "Whee-oo, the things you do to me. Now be a dear and sit somewhere while I throw something on."

I sat while she stretched out her legs and ran sheer blue nylons up over her white thighs, gartering them to the girdle. She was an attractive woman, I give her that; it was a joy to the eyes to watch her slide into a dress and add earrings and a bracelet. On the surface she was everything a man could want; underneath she was cold, heartless and sadistic.

It was a pleasant night, cool and invigorating. I drove slowly to Doctor Vance's office, wanting Felicia to savor the evening. This was to be her last night on earth. She sat with her head back, eyes closed, a little smile twitching the corners of her mouth. She had me right where she wanted me from now on, the way she had Dori Pierce and Doctor Vance. I belonged to her, fully and completely.

Felicia was the only patient. We went right into his inner office off which a door opened to a small laboratory where Doctor Vance sometimes mixed his own prescriptions. He had the tonic ready.

"Give you some right now," he said with a slight frown, "though you seem to have made a fine recovery." His eyes touched me. "Maybe David is all the medicine you needed."

He handed the bottle to her and she poured a teaspoonful, then a second as Vance was writing on a pad. "I want you to take another two spoonsful just before you retire. It won't keep you awake."

"Tastes sort of chocolatey," Felicia commented.

The doctor took the bottle and reached for a metal cap. He screwed it on and began shaking the bottle. "Remember to shake well before taking. Very important." He shook it a few more times, then slipped the bottle into a bag and handed it over.

At the car, Felicia held out her hand. "The keys, David. I feel like driving."

"But—"

Her purple eyes stared up at me. I wondered if she knew what was in the back of my mind; almost instantly, I told myself not to be a fool. The tonic was getting to her, filling her with energy. That was all.

"You bet," I agreed, and dropped the keys into her palm.

She drove expertly, just as she did everything else. Her slippered foot on the accelerator was a symbol to me of the way she went through life. People were like cars to her, to be taken over and handled, steered, braked and speeded up whenever the mood was on her. Cars were made for that sort of thing, but people were something else. People had feelings, and this Felicia Marr ignored.

"David, come closer," she said as she swung around a curve. I slid as close as I could. She wanted affection, or petting—you name it—so I figured it was up to me to give it to her, if only to keep her off balance. If she'd been suspicious of me, if I'd betrayed myself in some way, I wanted to convince her she was wrong.

There would be other nights when she could die.

I put my hands on her body and moved them around gently. In a way it was exciting enough. Felicia Marr was going to die. I was going to kill her. And here she was, soft and warm and hungry under my palms, squirming a little to the sensations exploding in her erogenous zones as I fondled her while she drove. Morbid, of course; but I was beyond caring about the niceties.

When she braked the car in the driveway she whispered, "Damn you!" with a sob in her voice and turned to me. I half lifted her in my arms, dragging her across the console to my kiss. She was breathing harshly and her breasts were as solid as two rocks on my chest. We played around for a few minutes, teasing one another. When we decided to call a halt and go up to her bedroom, her skirt was around her hips and her legs were fully revealed in their blue nylons, up as far as the pink girdle. Her thighs were very pale above the tight stocking tops, trembling gently as she let me tug her off the seat and out of the car.

"Hurry," she breathed. "Goddamnit, hurry!"

We ran for the house, up the front stairs, and burst into her bedroom. She was laughing softly in anticipation as she closed the door and threw the bolt. "There. Nobody can bother us now. We're alone again, lover."

She turned her back so I could run her zipper down. As the dress fell open I reached between the flaps and unhooked her brassiere. Felicia giggled and ran for the bathroom, holding the dress up in front of her.

140

"Get undressed, darling," she called back to me.

Orders from on high. I shrugged and slipped off my jacket. I was down to shorts, shoes and socks when the bathroom door opened. Felicia wanted her handbag.

"The damn tonic," she told me. "I'll take another slug now and get it out of the way."

I removed the bottle from her handbag and began shaking it as I carried it across the room. Her bare arm slid out, fingers widespread. I slipped the bottle between them. The door was ajar. I watched as she drank.

I found a pair of pajamas in a dresser drawer—she always kept a new pair on hand for the nights we spent together—and put them on. I threw back the covers and sat on the edge of the bed, waiting. It was up to Felicia to call the turns. As soon as I saw her, I would know what sort of routine it was going to be.

She came out after a while in a transparent red nightgown out of which her white shoulders and throat rose in gentle curves. She was a beautiful woman and the gold harem slippers on her feet added to her attractiveness.

She lifted her arms above her head, smiling faintly. "I am a succubus, a female devil," she announced. "You are a poor lost soul sent to me for torture." It was to be one of those nights, I thought; she would bring me to my knees before giving herself to me. "Lie down on the bed, David."

She intended driving me crazy with her caresses and her kisses. I would actually experience real pain before she would throw herself on me and bring the relief my body would need so desperately. It gave her a sense of power, the knowledge that she was wanted so fiercely that for me not to have her was an agony.

I lay back on the coverlets. Felicia came to stand beside the bed, looking down at me. There was a sadistic glitter in her eyes. She was going to punish me for carrying on with Renata Delabba, her eyes said.

Then her expression changed.

A spasm of pain touched her white face, altering it oddly. She put a hand on her belly and pressed it inward. She whimpered.

"David, I feel funny. I hurt—inside here."

She began bending over. Both hands were now fastened to her middle and she was gasping hoarsely. As if in slow motion, her body was folding at the knees, toppling forward. She was gasping for breath, mouth wide open. Her eyes were protruding and looked glassy, feverish. Her knees hit the carpet with a thump, so that her cheek rested on the edge of the bed.

She could not talk but made only mewling sounds. As I bent over her, I noticed a bloody froth on her lips.

"Felicia? What's wrong?" I asked stupidly.

I bent over her, took her in my arms, lifted her to the bed. A stomach cramp, I thought; and yet a part of my mind told me it was more serious than that. No stomach cramp caused such symptoms.

I left her writhing on the bed while I dialed. The phone rang and rang at the other end but no one answered. He must be on a call, I told myself. I went to the bedroom door and fumbled with the bolt, recalling how Felicia had locked it.

I ran downstairs and woke Mrs. Bennett by pounding on her door. I yelled for her to keep trying to raise Vance. Then I raced upstairs and woke Dori Pierce.

"Something's wrong with Felicia," I told her as she belted a bathrobe about her pajamas.

"I hope it's serious," she said dully.

It was serious. When we came into the bedroom we could see Felicia Marr's body twisted grotesquely as if frozen in a last convulsive jerk. Her eyes were open, staring. A thin line of blood trickled from her mouth.

Dori went to her, fumbling at a wrist.

Then she turned a white, frightened face up to me. "She's dead," she announced. "You stupid fool! Couldn't you have done it in some cleverer way?"

The police arrested me for murder. I had been the only person with her between the time we had been in Doctor Vance's office and the time she died. The fatal poison was potassium cyanide, dissolved in the medicine Doctor Vance had prepared. Since Vance had given her two teaspoonsful in his office, and since potassium cyanide acts within five minutes, the medicine had not been poisoned at that time. I was the only one who could have done it.

The police reconstructed it this way. We had entered her bedroom. Felicia had locked the door. After I had unzipped her dress and she'd gone into the bathroom, her handbag with the medicine bottle had been in the room with me. I had slipped the poison into it then, and given it to her when she asked for it.

She had taken the poison in the bathroom, then came into the bedroom to die in front of me. It was a good, neat case. Logically, it made sense. Nobody else could have done it but—the only thing was, I was innocent.

I could not prove that innocence.

At the trial, it was testified that Felicia Marr had caused me to be beaten up in Naples. This was my motivation for the murder, according to the prosecution. The state produced the three hoodlums who had done the job, the Italian doctor who had patched me up, one of the nurses who had taken care of me.

Doctor Vance took the stand to say he had prepared the medicine, that he had given it to Felicia in his office, that if it had been poisoned then she would have died before reaching home. Potassium cyanide works fast in the human body. Death comes anywhere from five to fifteen minutes after taking a fatal dose. Three grains is fatal.

The jury required less than half an hour to return its verdict. According to them, I was guilty of murder in the first degree.

The judge sentenced me to die. As I said when I started, I write this from the death cell.

I have told my story. I wanted to kill Felicia Marr, but I did not. I have tried to discover how she was poisoned but I have been unable to do so.

I am asking for help.

From anyone . . .

CLIPPING FROM THE WESTPORT *Town Crier*

Westport, Conn. A sensational new development in the recent trial of David M. Horne for the murder of wealthy business woman and socialite Felicia Marr occurred yesterday when Justice Julian Evans disclosed the receipt of a letter from Doctor Thurlow Vance, postmarked Brazil. Justice Evans presided at the recent murder trial.

Doctor Vance is the physician who prepared the tonic in which was placed the potassium cyanide that killed Mrs. Marr. Two days after the jury found Horne guilty of murder in the first degree, Doctor Vance married a Miss Elvira Bennett and left on an extended honeymoon cruise. He had sold his practice and intended living abroad, he said at that time.

The letter follows:

Dear Judge Evans,

This letter is written with the express purpose of exonerating David Horne of the murder of Felicia Marr. I am the guilty party—I alone. Enough was brought out about Felicia

143

Marr at the trial to reveal the fact that she was a cruel, grasping woman with a hold over practically everyone with whom she came in contact. She had such a hold over me.

I am not a young man. Too long have I permitted her to order me about like a slave, to prevent me from marrying the woman I love. It was time I freed myself and took the chance for happiness I feel I deserve.

Enough of that. Now as to my *modus operandi*.

The medicine was not poisoned when Felicia Marr drank it in my office. The poison was administered by means of the bottle cap, which was coated with enough potassium cyanide in crystal form to prove fatal once it was dissolved —by shaking—in the medicine. I shook it myself while in the office, after Felicia Marr had swallowed the tonic, to make certain the poison was in solution. It needed no further shaking, though David Horne also shook it up.

When I arrived at the house in response to a call from Elvira Bennett, I removed the bottle cap and substituted a clean one, to prevent anyone from detecting the presence of any crystals that might still adhere to it. Then I turned it over to the police.

I will not be back to the United States. I am taking a different name in the country where I intend living. I have quite a sizable fortune in cash, more than enough to live with Elvira in retirement.

Elvira and I both agreed that we did not want to start our life together with the death of David Horne on our consciences. Release him. He is innocent. Only I am guilty of the death of Felicia Marr. It is a guilt which I do not regret carrying the rest of my life.

Thurlow Vance.

David M. Horne will be released at once.

In a special interview, Mr. Horne had this to say, "I am extremely grateful to Doctor Vance. His murder method was so clever that unless he willingly came forward, no one could ever prove what he had done.

"My future plans? Well, you might say that I intend going to Italy. Like Doctor Vance, I have enough money to last me for a long time to come. I hope to be married. Her name is Renata. Her last name is unimportant because it will soon be Horne."

Horne was in good spirits.

He, too, will live abroad.

THE END